To Deborah

JOCKEYING FOR YOU

STACY HOFF

Pt. II of our fabulous authors' event

Stacy

SOUL MATE PUBLISHING

New York

JOCKEYING FOR YOU

Copyright©2016

STACY HOFF

Cover Design by Leah Kaye-Suttle

Published in the United States of America by

Soul Mate Publishing

P.O. Box 24

Macedon, New York, 14502

ISBN: 978-1-68291-239-3

ebook ISBN: 978-1-68291-234-8

www.SoulMatePublishing.com

To my family,

Eyal, Ryan, Aaron, Marilyn, and Michael,

Who always make me feel like I've come in first place.

Thanks for jockeying for me.

Acknowledgements

So many thanks need to be given for this book. Horse racing is a sport I initially knew nothing about, despite my life-long fascination with horses. In order to write this novel, I read everything I could about the topic. I also traveled up and down the state of New York, from Belmont Park to Saratoga Springs, to interview experts and see the different race tracks in person. Despite all these efforts, however, this story would not have come to life had it not been for the people below. Thank you for getting me over the finish line.

National Museum of Racing and Hall of Fame (Saratoga Springs, New York) for providing priceless expertise, fact-finding assistance, and enthusiasm for my project. Special recognition goes to their Historian, Allan Carter, and their Education Curator, Karen Wheaton.

Oklahoma Training Track (Saratoga Springs, New York) for providing information about life on the track, as well as giving me a wonderful tour.

Rhonda Lane for her expertise on the horse racing industry and allowing me to pester her with my endless questions.

Debby Gilbert (Founder and Senior Editor of Soul Mate Publishing, Inc.) for all her support and furthering my writing career. I am truly happy to have found a home with Soul Mate Publishing.

Dan Spiegel for maintaining my website, www.stacyhoff. com, with dogged diligence.

Judy Roth for her line-editing magic and valuable feedback.

Amina Connelly for being the most positive and encouraging beta reader an author could ever want.

Chapter 1

Ryder Hannon assessed the thoroughbred stallion in one of her stalls at New York City's Belmont Park, her blue eyes cool. "I think Golden Child is shying away from using his back hoof. Better have the vet check him out. I don't want him racing if he's in any pain."

"Already did," Lenny answered, his white beard stretched wide in a grin. The stooped-over man had five red strands of hair on his otherwise bald head. "I taught you to be a good trainer. But don't ever think you're smarter than the teacher."

Ryder pushed the bangs of her short blond bob away from her face and smiled back sheepishly. "Right. I should've guessed you'd have already sought the vet out."

"Yup. I wasn't in this business forty years for nothing." Lenny's gruff voice was laced with affection. "I got your father into horseracing. Way before you were even born. So don't be a hotshot at twenty-seven."

Ryder suppressed a smile. *Yes, Lenny, I know all about it.* If one of her horses fell on her head she couldn't forget it. Even if he hadn't told her this story a gazillion times, her father certainly had. Since her father had passed on, Lenny seemed to be doing double-time with family anecdotes to make up for the shortfall. Between the two men's tales, she could have written a biography of how Lenny had made her father an assistant trainer, training horses at the young age of seventeen.

The two men had become close, a de facto father-son relationship despite the lack of blood tie. They remained close even when her dad gave up the horse training business to become a jockey instead. Only to become one of the best horse racers ever. In fact, racing had turned her father, Philip Hannon, into a legend.

When Philip's only child, a girl, was born, the name "Ryder" was given with the expectation she would one day carry on the Hannon winning tradition. That was, to the extent any horse owner would consent to having a female jockey.

Lenny had done what he could to help Ryder become a jockey, too. As a trainer, Lenny was in an even better position than her father because trainers were responsible for picking which jockey was selected to ride. Owners didn't typically get involved in a trainer's selection, unless the stakes were real high, or they didn't like the trainer's choices.

As soon as Ryder turned eighteen, Lenny selected her as the jockey for a few small scale "under the radar," type races. Ones where the owners wouldn't bother to ask him too many questions. Within a short time, Ryder had successfully ridden enough low-dollar claiming races to obtain her jockey license and join the Jockey Guild.

But soon, word got out to the horses' owners about Lenny picking a female jockey. Her work dried up and she sat idle, busying herself with Lenny's training work and waiting for her next chance.

It wasn't until two years later, when Ryder turned twenty, her big chance came around. One owner, as a favor to both Lenny and her father, agreed to let her ride in a "fillies and mares three years old and upward maiden race." This relatively low scale race had been the opportunity of the lifetime until the horse tripped and fell on top of her. A serious concussion ended her racing career, at her doctor's insistence.

Ryder winced at the painful memory. Seven years later, she still had several physical scars from the fall. Rough, raised streaks of skin spread out under her ribs. At least she was alive. The eleven-hundred-pound horse could have killed her. As a trainer, she'd be safe.

Lenny and her mother were only too happy to have her pursue a safe, quiet life. But she would never know if her father would have wanted her to get back in the saddle. He had died shortly thereafter.

Lenny had been quick to step up more than before. He had made her a promise to turn his business over to her when she was ready. Ryder had clung to all of Lenny's instructions like a child would a teddy bear. She had mastered it all. Lenny realized this and took it as his cue to finally take a back seat in the business. The devoted old man had been true to his word.

For a full year now she had been running it. Lenny often fought his urge to get out of the back seat. Not easy for a man who loved control but who also loved her as the child he never had. Her gratitude for the seemingly gruff Lenny was without bounds.

"You're not going to get all sentimental, are you, Lenny?" Ryder pretended to admonish. "In my book it's too early in the morning to reminisce."

Lenny glanced at his watch. "Early? It's late. I can't believe it's 11:00 a.m. already." Grabbing Golden Child's reins he hurried to bring the stallion back to his stall. "I'd better go see what's holding up the doc." Moments later, Lenny was gone.

With any luck the vet would be there soon. Belmont Park's back of the house was nothing short of organized chaos this morning. The area behind the racetrack, closed off from the general public, was a heavily populated barn type area with lots of little buildings. People and horses went in and out of the backstretch like busy bees in a hive.

Several of her own horses were being hot walked after their workout. Other horses were being washed and rubbed down by groomsmen. Jockeys were checking with their agents to learn which horses would be ridden. Jockeys' valets were readying the gear for the afternoon's races. As a trainer, her own day would calm down once the races started. She'd get a chance to sit down and catch up on everything from paperwork to talking to owners. Maybe the to-do stack on her desk would even reduce a good amount.

Ryder turned to go back to her office when the sight of an imposing man caught her peripheral vision. She looked up, immediately noticing the man's height gave the horses some serious competition. Standing at five-foot one-inch tall, Ryder never felt so tiny. It was one thing to be short compared to a thoroughbred. Another to feel the same way around a man.

His broad shoulders and muscular frame—from what she could make of it underneath the light blue oxford shirt and black slacks he wore—was no less imposing. Had the man not worn a dark expression, his handsome face would have been first to receive praise. His thin, yet well-formed lips were slightly downturned. His dark, mid-length hair was brushed away from his face, showing dark eyes that warned of an impending storm. The handsome yet imposing appearance made Ryder feel immediately physically attracted yet cautious.

Another temperamental owner. Just what I need. "Can I help you?" Ryder asked in her most professional voice.

"That depends on whether you're Ryder Hannon. Are you?"

"Yep. You found me. What can I do for you, Mr. . . .?"

"Carter. Jake Carter." The man raked a hand through his hair. "Can we go somewhere to talk?"

"I'm not usually in the habit of going off with strangers. But I've heard of you, Mr. Carter. You own a heck of a lot of excellent horses. We can sit down and talk business. I didn't know you wanted a new trainer."

"Yes. I need to hire rather quickly. I've been checking out a few people. I hear you've got some particular talents that could serve my newest horse well."

Ryder's eyebrow arched. "What talents are those?"

"Are you willing to talk, or not?"

"Sure. We can chat in my office. Things ought to be calmer for me around one o'clock. Is that too late for you? It'll give us about an hour before post-time if one of your horses is racing today."

He shook his head. "I don't have a race on today. You?"

"Yes, one. But not until almost three o'clock so most of my afternoon is free and clear."

"Excellent. We'll have lunch at the Turf and Field Club. I have a regular table there so ask for me. See you then."

The track's VIP restaurant. Figures. A first for me. "Sure. Bye," Ryder said softly. She doubted the man heard her. He was already down the path.

Jake surveyed the floor-to-ceiling windows of the Turf and Field Club, the track's members only restaurant. Good for him to score such a coveted table. It paid to tip well. Keeping the wait staff happy was easy to do if one could afford it. Luckily, he could. The number of races his thoroughbred horses won kept him in the black. Not easy to accomplish in an industry where profits were about as stable as earthquakes. One bad investment could easily create a profit pit. An avalanche of bills. And eventually, business obliteration. The trick was to invest wisely. Both with the horses he bought and with the staff he hired.

Whether Ryder Hannon was going to join his staff as a trainer was unclear. He'd talk to her over lunch and see if she lived up to her outstanding reputation. Of course, there would be no definitive way to know how good she was until she actually started working with Handsome Dancer.

If she could pull off successfully training his wayward horse, she'd be the first. Of all the horses he'd bought, Handsome's prospect had become the ugliest. Despite having the greatest potential of any horse he had owned. It'd take somebody truly special, unique, and very patient to train the untrainable. Handsome Dancer's spirit was as wild as it was strong.

Could the same be said for the potential new trainer? Ryder Hannon was a tiny thing, stature-wise. But she had to have a lot of guts and spirit herself to have been a jockey. Not only was the sport incredibly dangerous, it was quite rare to have a woman among their ranks. Not because women weren't capable of doing the job. No, it was because most horse owners were male and insisted on having other men jockey. For a woman to be selected was an accomplishment unto itself. Ryder not only had the right racing pedigree but an invaluable skill set in her own right. One he needed. Because if Handsome Dancer couldn't stop throwing jockeys off his back like some kind of bucking bronco, then whatever potential the horse had would be for naught.

Handsome's failure would be more than an income tax loss. It would be a loss of something he actually believed in. Every instinct screamed Handsome Dancer was something special. From lineage to perfect body form—everything but personality—Handsome Dancer was the secret weapon he'd been longing for.

Not that anyone agreed with him. Handsome had been initially put up in a cheap sixteen-thousand-dollar claiming race by his prior owner. Worse, there were no claims for Handsome for even that meager amount. Then Handsome lost his race when he refused to leave the starting gate. The owner was then ready to accept any price someone would pay for him.

Jake's ears pricked up when he heard Ryder's voice. Upon seeing her, his eyes grew wide. The woman had changed out of her leggings and mucky boots and now wore a form-flattering dress. *Speaking of perfect body build.* The slim but attractive curves on her tiny frame were beautifully enhanced by the dress' simple tailoring. Despite being unquestionably athletic, she was definitely a woman. The open-toed sandals she wore had a high heel, giving height to her tiny stature. Her blond bob hung loose around her face, shining with the same bright gleam as a freshly groomed horse's mane. Her blue eyes were made more dramatic by a new application of eyeliner.

If she was trying to impress him on looks alone, it was working. He'd have to make sure to focus on her words instead of her pretty mouth. But he wasn't here to woo women. When money and his dream were on the line, priorities had to be placed where they mattered. On the horse.

Jake stood up from the chair as the maître d' walked her over. She thanked him with a soft voice and sat down. The maître d' left.

"You sure you can control a horse with a soft voice like that?" Jake asked, half-teasing.

He could tell she was sizing up his comment, whether it was a joke or an admonishment. Rather than help her out, he decided to see what she'd make of it.

"They don't call me the *horse whisperer* for nothing," she finally let out with an accompanying shrug.

He smiled. *Good. She can hold her own. With Handsome Dancer, she'll need to. He won't explain himself, either.*

"Glad you brought that up. Tell me a little about your philosophy."

"All right. I imagine you've already heard a bit about how I train or we wouldn't be talking. My approach is simple, I help the horse train himself."

Jake felt his eyebrows furrow. "Excuse me? What?"

Ryder frowned.

One of his regular waiters approached, pen and paper already out. "Give us a minute, Robert?" Turning his attention back to her, he asked, "I'm sorry, you were explaining your philosophy. It sounded very . . . unorthodox."

"I'm guessing you've seen my track record, so I'm confident *unorthodox* works. I don't treat a horse like it's some kind of four-footed magical carpet, ready to take off at our command. Horses are live creatures. They let us command them when they want to. And if they don't, no amount of breaking them is going to win a race."

She paused, cleared her throat, then picked up the glass of ice water in front of her and took a sip. She was peering at him thoughtfully over the rim of the glass. "It's not as crazy as it sounds. I simply believe a horse that wants to win will do its best to do so. A horse that doesn't, won't. The jockey can use the whip dozens of time. It won't matter. A horse may go a little faster to stop being struck, but it won't pull out its last reserve of energy to win. That's why I don't have my jockeys use a whip on a regular basis. They're only allowed to use it for the horse's own safety, like to prevent it from bumping into another horse or a guardrail."

Jake felt his brow furrow deepen. "Without using a whip, how does the horse know when it's time to go all-out for the home stretch?"

Ryder met his steady gaze. "Of course, a lot of jockeys use whips to let the horse know when to go faster. But it seems redundant to me. Why use a whip when it already knows from the jockey's body language what it needs to do?"

His eyebrow was now arching. "Body language?"

"Sure. Like when the jockey gets lower in the saddle and leans all the way forward to hang on the horse's neck, the horse knows it's the home stretch. When the jockey is straighter in the saddle at the beginning, the horse knows not to use up his strength too fast."

With every word coming out of her mouth, he liked her better and better. Though the jockeys he knew never struck a horse to hurt, only to spur the animal on, it wasn't a practice he was a fan of. The best riders were more apt to hand ride at the end, a humane—and more effective way, to his mind—of encouraging the animal to give its last burst of energy toward the finish line. Still, he'd never heard of using no whip at all. But he wasn't here to discuss his philosophy, he was here to discuss hers. "You've got pretty unique ideas, I'd say."

"Maybe." She shrugged again, her tan shoulders exposed in the brightly colored sundress. "I think my way is best, not only for the horse but the owner as well. A happy horse is a winning horse."

Someone actually agrees with me. Amazing. I should stick her comment in the other owners' faces. He took a long, hard breath. "How about a horse that will be especially difficult to train? Still think you can do it without going about it the standard way?"

He watched her take another sip of water. It looked like she was considering the question in full measure.

"Yes," she said eventually. "I think a horse that's difficult to train may have some emotional issues. I'd definitely want to use a soft touch on a horse like that."

The waiter came back to them to take their drink order. Jake motioned for her to go first.

"I'll stick with the ice water. Thanks," she replied.

"Do you want anything to eat? Since I'm the one interviewing, I'm buying." He allowed himself to give her a smile.

"Thank you. I guess I have time for a salad before I have to go back to work."

He quirked up an eyebrow. "That's it? Are you sure?"

She nodded. "A Waldorf salad, please. Dressing on the side."

"Okay Robert, you heard the lady. I'll get the filet mignon. Medium rare."

"Very good, sir. Right away," the waiter replied before hustling toward the kitchen.

"When I'm hungry," Jake said wryly, "nothing gets done, so I hope you don't suffer the same way. I feel like I'm eating with a jockey."

"Since I used to be one, you kind of are. I still have a 'eat light' mentality. I think it's ingrained at this point. I don't notice what I'm missing because I'm not used to having it anyway."

"I heard about your racing record."

He could see her body tense up. "My fall was a mistake. A jockey's mistake. But I don't make mistakes as a trainer."

"Relax, I didn't say what I heard about your past was bad. I heard you were quite good until your accident." He observed her lips were tight. A straight line of pressed flesh.

"I focus on the future, not the past," she answered. "Both in my life and in my profession." Her voice was courteous but clipped.

Clearly, he had hit a bump with her. If she were any tenser she could be a filly at the starting gate for the first time. "Well, we can talk about jockeying later." He observed her nod slowly. No matter how tense she was, this was one business lunch he didn't want to end.

Ryder hardly ate the delectable Waldorf salad in front of her, picking at the lettuce as if she were back to being a fussy eater in second grade. Why had she mentioned anything about having been a jockey? He had made only a light reference to riding and she cringed as if he'd thrown a bucket of cold water over her.

An image sprang into her head, the memory of it colder and wetter. The afternoon of her fall. Track conditions deteriorating from a downpour that would not let up. All that morning anxiously awaiting updated weather reports, none of them getting any better. Thunder and lightning setting in. Flashes bright enough to light up the black sky. Thunder loud enough to sound like God himself was snapping a jockey's whip. Wind and sheets of rain pouring in with such intensity the atmosphere was no more than an electrically charged blur.

Ten minutes later, the storm had stopped. The skies cleared to a dull gray a few hours before the races. The track had dried out enough for the authorities to allow the race to go on but posted on the board the track conditions were 'poor.'

Ryder had almost bitten her lip off in indecision. She knew she was largely untested in poor conditions. The horse she was on had some experience on muddy turf, though, so she had taken the calculated risk. But hadn't calculated enough. Five minutes before the bugle sounded the rain came down once again. Within moments of the downpour the track's status was downgraded from 'poor' to 'sloppy.'

Wet earth quickly turning into mini rivers. Face stinging from cold rain. And then falling as the horse went down, tripped by the horse in front of it . . .

"Um, Ryder? You okay? You look a bit pale."

"Oh. Sorry. I'm fine, really. Just feeling a little cold is all. The air conditioning in here is nice. I'm not used to it." She laughed nervously. "The stables are like a big oven it's so hot in there."

Her lips stretched out into a smile she hoped would put him at ease. *Why am I reliving such an old memory?* For someone who espoused not dwelling in the past, she was hardly living up to her own words.

"Would you like my jacket?" Jake offered, already getting up to shrug it off.

"You're very sweet, but I'll be fine."

She ate quickly, more for the distraction than to ease hunger. *Geez, what is wrong with me?*

At least the subsequent downturn in her conversation hadn't hampered his meal. The thick steak he'd ordered was disappearing at a fast clip. A man who could relish a good meal and still maintain a physique like his was a man to be admired. Judging by the envious stares from several women at a nearby table, Ryder wasn't alone in this theory. Through his oxford shirt, she could make out a sleek, muscular body. If Jake had been a horse, no doubt he would have been a thoroughbred.

She glanced at him and swallowed through a tight throat. "I'm sorry. I shouldn't have been curt. You were polite about my riding past. More than you should have been, given the outcome."

He put his fork down. "Sorry our conversation got off-track."

Despite her tension, she laughed. "Good pun."

He cocked his head for a minute, as if he were trying to catch her meaning. A moment later, he grinned. "It was inadvertent. Glad you're quick witted. Handsome Dancer's trainer will have to be. That horse is going to be a handful."

"I'll be happy to take on the challenge. Tell me more about him."

He shoved his empty plate aside and leaned toward her. "To be honest, he's a conundrum. He's got great lineage. His sire is Handsome Winner, who won the Belmont Stakes. His dam is Dancing Wind, who did exceptionally well in three-year-old-and-older mare races."

"Which one of his parents do you own?"

"Neither. I don't pay for breeding rights. Too much risk in what the foal is going to be like. Besides, I don't like to race them until they're ready, nearer to their third birthday, like Handsome Dancer. Waiting that long for my investment to pay off is too risky. Besides, the foal may not have any racing ability, and then I have a lost leader."

Ryder felt her tight lips relax and a slight smile break out. A man who refused to race young horses was not only a good owner but a good person. Racing horses barely at their second birthday was way too young for the majority of these animals in her opinion. Unfortunately, some owners were tempted to race horses as soon as possible, regardless of the animal's condition, for the potential of fast returns. Horseracing was an expensive business. And buying a breeding session was one of the most dangerous. A few thousand dollars for the breeding, the vet bills for pregnancy and birth, plus the costs of the foal's upkeep for years until it was ready to race.

Assuming the foal would ever be ready to race. Like human babies, foals could be born with any type of physical issue. With horses, however, the tiniest little imperfection could mark the foal as a lost cause.

"When did you get Handsome Dancer?" she asked.

"I bought him four months ago from Barney Smythe."

She could feel her nose wrinkle.

He let out a sharp laugh. The masculine sound was beautifully baritone. "I guess you know him."

I hate that my face is so easy to read. She hesitated for a second. "I know *of* him." The most she was going to admit.

"Yeah, he doesn't have the best reputation. But I got Handsome Dancer for a song. Barney was ready to give him away. But Handsome should be ready to get down to business now. Though his prior trainer got nowhere with him."

"Why not?"

"Handsome is wild. Barney thought he was untrainable and I understand why. Handsome didn't want to be broken. Still doesn't. He likes to throw riders off of him. And when he does allow someone to ride him he is very obstinate. He'll start, then stop. Won't increase his speed. Things like that."

She could feel her forehead wrinkle. "If that's that case, what makes you think he has potential?"

"The few times he's been willing to practice on the track, his time is outstanding. He can easily do six furloughs in a minute-point-nine. And that's with him completely unconditioned and untrained. Imagine what he can do with proper workouts and guidance. This horse could be a legend. I can't let an opportunity like this pass me by."

She nibbled on her lower lip as she contemplated this. "His time for an untrained horse is impressive, certainly. What are other people saying?"

He gave her a flat stare. "I'm the owner. What do I care what anybody else thinks?"

"I'm trying to get a full picture of Handsome Dancer. The fuller the picture, the better the assessment. I don't want to take your money or your time if I can't do any better with him."

"That's a first."

"What is?"

"Someone concerned about taking my money or my time. It's nice to see." He gave her a warm smile.

In any other circumstance it would have made her toes curl.

"To be honest," he continued, "all the owners I know think I'm nuts. In fact, anyone who knows this horse thinks I'm nuts. Barney Smyth sold him for a song for a solid reason. But I think they're all wrong. And I'm willing to pay you a nice base salary to prove it."

"Has the racing association threatened to take away his gate card?"

"Yes, though thankfully Handsome recovered before he had to go back to school."

"What about your family? What do they think?"

She saw him blink, taken aback. Then he laughed. "If I were married, maybe my wife would think I'm crazy, too. My only sibling, Dina, is supportive of what I do, generally. But not this time. She hasn't seen Handsome Dancer yet but doesn't seem too enthused from my description. My mom isn't around anymore."

Jake lowered his voice and stared out the enormous window. "Dina likes to try to fill in for mom. She means well, of course, but at thirty-five years old she's way too young to live the role. Go tell her that, though. Good luck. Fortunately her husband and kids take some of her attention off me."

Ryder felt herself smiling again. "What's your dad think about the horse?"

Jake's gaze turned back to her, his voice flat. "Let's just say he's not real enthused about putting money into anything that's not a sure bet."

Ryder nodded sympathetically. "I see. I did a Google search on you and your family before coming here." She fought back the blush threatening to rush forth. "Standard practice before I take on an owner I'm unfamiliar with." She let out an uncomfortable cough. "It seems your father can be quite . . . opinionated."

Jake's laugh was even flatter. "If you're referring to the articles when he openly said disparaging things about one of my horses right before the Belmont Stakes, then yes, he can be very opinionated." He straightened up in his chair. "People can think what they want. I know what *I* think. I don't like people telling me *no* if I believe the answer is really *yes*." Leaning forward in his chair, he said, "You must agree with me. You never would have been a jockey if you didn't. There must be tons of people who told you a woman can't do it."

She blinked in wonderment. Until now there were less than a handful of people who understood what she had had to endure being a female jockey. Her mother. Lenny. Mindy. Her father, when he was alive. Adding someone to this list would have been unthinkable. Especially if that person was an owner. And as stunning as Jake. "I understand. I've had plenty of people try to shut me down."

His grin was as bright as the afternoon sun shining

through the restaurant's huge windows. "So we have that in common. Good to know you can relate."

"I do. I'm sure we'll get along great, if you hire me."

His grin was lopsided now, as if toying with her. "When you say *we* will get along great, do you mean me and you, or do you mean you and Handsome Dancer?"

She felt her face go hot.

He laughed loudly. "Either way," he said, not waiting for her to respond, "I'm glad you think so. Why don't I bring Handsome around to make sure you'll get along with him?"

She nodded and begged her blush to lighten. "Okay. Later this afternoon?"

"Around four o'clock?"

"Yes. Great. See you then."

They rose from their seats and shook hands.

"Yes. Later," he agreed.

Ryder left, excited about the opportunity to see two handsome males return.

Chapter 2

Time flew until four o'clock. Ryder barely noticed the hours rushing by. Calls to owners, instructions to jockeys for future races, and one passive-aggressive argument with a surly jockey's valet all ate time at a fast pace. But her best, albeit most time-consuming, distraction was her four-year-old mare, Yankee Doodle Girl, winning her race. Yankee hadn't exactly been a long shot, but the mare hadn't been thought to win, either. Ryder almost laughed at the thought that she and Yankee had a lot in common—they both shouldn't be underestimated.

Better yet, Ryder would be getting ten-percent of Yankee's winnings. The ten percent bonus would be gladly accepted. The more races won, the more money Ryder had to rent stalls from the racetrack. Having more stalls meant more horses under her care. And more horses meant more chances of winning ten percent. Technically, when a trainer agreed to work with a horse, they were gambling, too.

That was, assuming the trainer had the luxury to decide which horses to train. Some trainers had a heck of a time convincing owners to—figuratively—bet on them. Though Ryder was in solid shape with nine stalls, she knew better than to take her luck for granted.

It seemed Jake was seriously considering betting on her. If they made a deal, and Handsome Dancer became a consistent winner and notable name, she'd have good leverage with the track to give her as many stalls as the best trainers around.

Ryder's ears honed in on the sound of approaching footsteps. She turned around, already looking up to spot the tall height of Jake. Instead, it was Mindy Gomez, one of the two other women trainers. Mindy wore her usual work attire, worn out blue jeans and stained gray sweatshirt. A long, brown braid hung over her left shoulder making the middle-aged woman appear youthful.

"Great job with Yankee Doodle back there, Ryder. I thought for sure you'd be screwed when your mare got stuck with the number one gate."

"Thanks, Mindy. I always cringe when they wind up in there. You know how the first horse loaded into the starting gate is usually the first to freak out."

Mindy lowered her voice and moved her eyes around the stalls to see if anyone was listening. "How did you calm Yankee Doodle Girl down? What's your trick?"

Ryder bit back a grin. Lenny had taught her everything she needed to know. Trainers in general were very secretive of their winning techniques. But Lenny had been only too happy to bestow on her every method and trick he had. Because if one of her horses failed to consistently place, another trainer would be hired in a heartbeat. Thankfully, the horses she trained performed well. Yankee Doodle Girl's win was not an anomaly.

Before Ryder could answer, Mindy shot out, "Wow. Check out Mr. Gorgeous."

Ryder's brow wrinkled. She didn't know any horse by the name of "Mr. Gorgeous."

She turned to peer down the path and quickly realized Mindy was referring to a man. Jake. He was, however, leading a horse that had to be the animal equivalent of a gorgeous man. In fact, both males truly were stunning. "The man is Jake Carter. The horse is Handsome Dancer. Mr. Carter wants me to check him out for possible training."

Mindy burst out laughing. "Training which one of those studs? I hope for your sake it's the man."

Ryder bit back a burst of laughter. Sure, Mindy was funny but laughing like a lunatic would not portray her as a professional when Jake arrived.

"Better yet," Mindy continued with a wicked grin, "forget you, I'm willing to take Jake Carter for a ride."

"Mindy, cut it out, will you? This is business." Ryder frowned. "And that was way too much information anyway."

Mindy laughed harder. "Hey, you asked."

"I didn't ask," Ryder shot back, crossing her arms over her chest. "Are you going to act crazy around him or will you pretend to be a normal person?"

Lenny suddenly appeared from a stall so quietly Ryder jumped in surprise. "Act normal around who?"

"Lenny! Stop popping up like that," Ryder protested. "Why don't you ever say when you're in the stall next to us?"

Mindy squinted at him. "How is it you don't make any noise?" she accused. "I swear, you're more ghost than guy."

Lenny grew taller and puffed out his chest like a rooster. "I don't need to explain myself to you, missy. I'm old enough to be your father."

"And you're short and sneak up on people." Mindy put her hands on her hips. "You're a leprechaun. Admit it."

Red smoke was going to come out of his ears. Just as soon as his face finished morphing into a tomato.

"She's only kidding," Ryder hastily said, putting a hand on him. "Mindy's a real joker today."

She could see Lenny taking a deep breath in an obvious attempt to calm down. "You ladies didn't answer my question. I asked who you're supposed to act normal around."

Mindy gestured to the fast-approaching Jake Carter. "Him," she answered, not waiting for Ryder to respond.

"That's Mr. Carter all right," Lenny said. "A man with a

whole lot of horses and a lot of influence on racing. Get lost, Mindy, will you? Ryder and I have some business to do."

Mindy laughed, waved, then disappeared somewhere down the long line of stalls. "We'll talk later, Ryder. See ya tomorrow. And you'd better spill all the details."

Jake entered, his brows furrowed. "Is now a bad time? I don't want to stop you from your other business, and it seems like you still have lots of activity going on."

Jake seriously hoped Ryder was free to talk. And not only about business. The way she blended in with this mostly male environment, while still retaining her femininity, was enough to intrigue him. Her body was petite yet appeared strong. Her personality seemed to match. Soft spoken, yet she could hold her own. He brushed back his too personal thoughts and demanded his brain focus on business.

"Yes, I'm free to talk now," Ryder answered. Her words seemed to be tossed out without much thought to him, her attention focused purely on his colt. "Hi, Handsome Dancer, let me take a look at you."

Her words sounded as soft as a summer breeze. No wonder people called her the horse whisperer.

"His name suits him well," she commented. "He *is* quite handsome." She checked him over thoroughly. Her eyes and hands gently and quickly darted over Handsome's body. Occasionally the horse's skin would flinch as her hands glided over him. Otherwise he stayed still.

"I'm surprised he's letting you touch him so easily," Jake marveled. "To be honest, he isn't nearly so docile for anyone else."

"He walked nice enough with you," she countered.

"Yeah," Jake said, scratching his head and letting out a laugh. "I think he likes me. But I can't ride him or train him, so it doesn't solve my problem."

"Horses are very sensitive to people. They either like someone or they don't." She used a higher-pitch murmur to address the horse. "Isn't that right, babycakes?"

After the horse stilled for a moment, it turned its head to nuzzle her shoulder. Its broad, open forehead had a snip of white on its nose. Jake watched Ryder's left hand immediately rise to stroke the long nose. With her other hand she continued to feel around the animal. What she was gauging, Jake wasn't sure. Whatever it was, Handsome was happy to have her check. The horse closed his large, clear brown eyes in apparent bliss and nuzzled her harder. In response, Ryder gave him more soft coos.

Moments later, she straightened and walked away for a moment, only to return with a carrot. "May I?" she asked Jake.

Handsome's ears perked up. Jake could swear the horse smiled. "Fine, go ahead. If I said no, Handsome would hate me, too."

She laughed softly. "He's a lover, not a fighter. He's got a bad rap."

If he wasn't careful, Ryder would be hypnotizing him with the same effortless moves as she was now using to control Handsome.

But then he watched her pat Handsome's head as he ate the carrot, her strokes long, circular, and obviously soothing. *Damn, if she keeps doing that with her hands I'll want to be a lover and not a fighter too.* He shook his head against the erotic thoughts, belatedly hoping she didn't notice.

Whatever emotions he was feeling, or fighting, were ones not shared by Ryder. She was doing a much better job staying on task. The questions she asked him and the comments she made were clearly geared toward work.

"He's in excellent shape," she remarked.

"I know. With what I pay for his upkeep, he should be."

"Mmmm, okay, but I didn't mean that. I mean his body. He's shaped perfectly. Even his chestnut color is right. The only quirk in his coloring are his white lower legs."

"I know. Is it true that a thoroughbred having white legs is an indicator the horse is no good? It was one of the many reasons the prior owner didn't want him anymore. And I've had plenty of people tell that to me, too."

"I personally don't believe it, no. I think it's a silly superstition. Horses with white patches on their heads aren't written off as failures. Plenty of thoroughbreds have snips or star patterns on their heads and nobody complains about that. So why the legs?"

She circled Handsome who was dutifully chewing the last of the carrot. "Finished so soon," she teased. She looked up at Jake. "Mind if I give him a candy? It'll keep him in a good mood while I continue."

"Do what you need to do."

She nodded and withdrew a striped peppermint candy from her jeans. When she unwrapped it she placed the hard candy on the flat of her hand. Handsome's lips descended, apparently eager to try it. While the horse was busy enjoying his sugar high, Ryder went about her inspection.

"His withers are perfectly formed." She picked up his back left hoof, which the horse easily gave her. "His feet are in great condition, too. They point straight ahead."

Jake observed her examining the hoof prints Handsome had made walking in, and then watched her move a few paces down to follow them. "Yep. He's not pigeon-toed, or pointed out. His tracks are dead parallel. And the hoofs are well sized for his body. If anything, they're a little bit wide, which is good. Narrow footed hooves can make a horse lame from having to bear too much load on these fast, hard tracks." She checked each hoof and then stood in front of the animal. "No sign of fractures in any of the hooves, either."

"I don't know whether to be impressed or wonder if you have a foot fetish." He almost laughed at her gaping expression.

After a moment, she smiled. "That's a bit personal, don't you think?"

Though her response was meant in the same jest as his question, it had the unexpected effect of a tightening in his pants. *No, it wasn't too personal at all.* He straightened up. "Only kidding, of course. What's up though with you and Handsome's hooves?"

She bit her lip, obviously thinking how best to respond. When she made that adorable face, it made his body respond as well.

"I'm going to try an analogy here. Are you into car racing?" she asked.

"No, I stick with horses. But since I drive a Ferrari you can try me anyway."

He lost his smile as she bit her lip again. Hopefully she was impressed and not put off. Otherwise, the Ferrari was going back to the dealer.

"Well, think of a horse's hooves like the tires on your Ferrari. No matter how awesome the vehicle itself is, it can't perform well on bad tires." She ran a hand down Handsome's front legs. "The rest of the animal's legs are important, too. For example, this joint, right above the hoof. He's got a nice short pastern on his two front legs so he won't exert as much strain on his tendons as long pasterns would. His hind leg pasterns are normal length, so there's no problem there."

Jake wondered if she would notice if he skimmed over her with the same detail she was observing Handsome. Hopefully not. It was too hard not to check out Ryder. The way she evaluated the horse was more than as an intelligent, interested, knowledgeable professional. She seemed to be so caught up it was as if she was in love. Whether her love affair was with her career in general or Handsome Dancer in particular he didn't know. He was starting to wish this captivating woman would look at him the same way.

Her hand ran up to the knees. "Normal forelegs, not *tied-in* or *calf-kneed*. Maybe a bit *over at the knee*, but this shouldn't be a problem at all." She switched her attention to the hind legs. "Hocks are good, too. His legs drop straight down from them, which is ideal. The back hooves aren't forward of the hocks, so we don't have a sickle or cow hock problem."

Jake liked how Ryder used the term "we." The woman had clearly said the inclusive term without giving it a second thought. Maybe she really did think they were a team. Hiring her seemed more like a sure bet with every minute he knew her.

"And how about these shoulders," Ryder marveled. "They're long and sloping. Pared with short cannons and long forearms, Handsome must have a very long stride. Powerful, too." She straightened and smiled at him, giving Jake a warm feeling. "Height and weight?"

Jake felt the warm feeling slip away and frowned. "Fifteen hands. Nine hundred and seventy-five pounds. Too small?"

"No. He's not that big, but a smaller horse like him can be more nimble. They can pick their ways through the narrow holes in the traffic jam on the way to the home stretch. Large horses can't slip through so easily. And Handsome's more lithe and lanky than blocky and big, which means he'll have more staying power even if it does mean less sprinting ability."

Handsome gently bumped his head against Ryder's shoulder in an obvious attempt to get her attention. She laughed and once again ran her hands up the horse's face. "The position of his ears is forward facing and alert. No nervous twitching or lying flat back like he's an angry guy."

She gave a scratch behind an ear and cooed, "You're not angry, are you, babycakes?"

"So you think the problem with him so far has been personality conflict?"

"I don't want to be rash or too harsh in my assessment, but I think it's a real possibility."

"As far as I know, no one's mistreated him."

"I'm sure they didn't. But again, horses are like people. Haven't you ever met anybody you just didn't like? For whatever reason? The minute you saw that person you instinctively wanted to turn around and leave?"

Jake did his best to mask his expression. *If she only knew the half of it.* "I might know what you're talking about."

"If you want me for the job I'm up to it. Handsome Dancer and I are sure to have more than a working relationship. We'll have a *real* relationship."

As if on cue, Handsome snorted and took a step closer to her. Ryder lifted a hand and stroked his face.

Jake had to admit he was a bit envious. "You're hired," he said, words flying out without thought or hesitation.

She put her hand on her chest as if surprised. "Glad to hear it," she said after a moment, then smiled. "Let's go back to my office to complete some paperwork." She called out Lenny's name.

Lenny appeared with his usual soundless pop-up aplomb. "What?"

Jake scrutinized the older man's expression, gratified when recognition took hold.

"Mr. Carter," the older man said in gruff acknowledgment before glancing back at Ryder. "He hiring you?"

"Yes, he is. Handsome Dancer is going to stay with us for a while."

Lenny nodded and directed himself to Jake. "If anybody can train 'em, my girl Ryder can." Taking Handsome Dancer gently by the reins, the man left without a further ado. "I'm going to walk him around. See how he takes to me."

Ryder apologized as soon as the old man was out of earshot. "That's Lenny Godfried. He's been in this business for forty years. He's like a father to me, although I'm sorry he was a little gruff." Despite the light chastisement, her affection for him seemed as deep as it was sincere. "He's a wonderful person, although he does seem tough. He's like your horse. People mistake him for being difficult when he's really a softy down inside."

Jake's mouth hung open at her words. Maybe Ryder was capable of reading more than horses. Maybe she could read people, too. If so, she would be a rare find. Someone willing to pierce the depths instead of staying superficially at the surface. If he knew more people like her, maybe he would be more accepted himself. Accepted for who he was instead of what he had. He was so much more than merely a man with money. "All right, we'll do the paperwork, and then I'll leave Handsome here. That is assuming you have a stall ready for him."

"I don't, but I can probably have one ready for him in a few days, if that's acceptable. I'll have to speak to the track."

He noted her pallor seemed ashen. He knew stalls were at a premium. Getting an extra one was no easy task. "If I get you a stall by tomorrow, can you start with Handsome then?"

She audibly gasped. "Well, sure. But . . ."

"No *buts*. If you're willing to do it, the problem of getting space is mine."

He almost laughed at her wide, open-mouthed expression. "Let's get on with the paperwork, shall we?"

"Why, yes. Of course. Thank you for entrusting Handsome Dancer to me."

He nodded. Heck, at this pace, he was tempted to trust himself to her, too.

Chapter 3

The next morning, Ryder had put Golden Child back in his stall when an even more impressive stallion appeared. The sight almost took her breath away. She unconsciously lifted a hand to smooth down her blond bob and ran her tongue quickly over her teeth. Finally she cleared her throat to get out words without gasping. "Good morning, Jake."

For some reason he kept shifting around. Odd, since his casual slacks and collared tee shirt should be comfortable. And expensive. The polo pony on his chest fit right in with the horse motif.

"Anything wrong?" she inquired.

"No. Do I seem antsy? I'm waiting on Emanuel Velazquez to get here. He's due in a few minutes."

Ryder went through a mental roster of names but came up blank on this one. "Who's Emanuel Velazquez?"

"The jockey I want for Handsome Dancer. He rides mostly out in the California tracks. Spent last year at Santa Anita. He'll be a good bet for Handsome. He's known to have a calm, sure way with skittish horses. Gets them to focus and do their best. I want to see how he and Handsome interact. If I'm going to make a go of this, I've got to see that all my players are in place."

I feel like a chess piece. Ryder nodded but said nothing. The jockeys around here wouldn't be thrilled to have an outsider riding a good horse, especially for a wealthy, well-connected horse owner. The better the horse, the better their own potential purse since a jockey would claim ten percent of a race's prize money for placing first. Since trainers picked the jockeys, Ryder reasonably guessed she'd become unpopular fast. Sure, she could blame Jake for the selection, but that would mean throwing him under the bus. The idea didn't sound appealing either on a personal or a professional level.

"I'll be happy to meet him," she answered with a smile she hoped wasn't too unsure.

"Good. I'm pleased to tell you I got you your stall. Handsome Dancer should be arriving here around three o'clock."

Her eyebrows shot up. "He is? You did?" She felt herself wince and immediately shut up. *I must sound like a moron.*

Instead of treating at her with derision for her childlike outburst, he gave a large grin. "You're impressed, huh?"

"Quite frankly, yes. You can pull off the impossible. It must be good to be king."

He roared with laughter. "Quite." He composed himself after a minute and gave her a look that seemed rich with meaning. "No queen though. Yet."

Ryder felt her face flush. Not knowing how to respond, she chose the business route. "I'll be here at three o'clock sharp to get Handsome set up. And please tell Emanuel to find me when he gets the chance."

"Will do." Jake walked away before she had a chance to babble on, which was good. Unfortunately, his fast departure left her feeling surprisingly empty.

"Will do what?"

Ryder was startled at the sudden question and whirled around to find Mindy standing there. "Can you stop doing that?" Ryder demanded.

"Doing what?" Mindy blinked innocently.

"Popping up out of nowhere."

Mindy shook her head. "You're mistaking me for Lenny. He's the one who pops up out of nowhere. Me, on the other hand, I walk over to you in these big ol' boots, noisy as all get-out. You're just too caught up in Mr. Gorgeous to have heard me."

"I'm sure that wasn't it. We were talking business."

"For someone talking business you were looking pretty misty-eyed. Admit it. Jake Carter is hot."

True to form, Lenny appeared from around a corner. The dark, wet spots on his denim shirt and pants made it clear he'd been washing down horses. "Mindy, don't you have something to do? I know Ryder does. She's got a ton of business to attend to. *All* business."

"Good luck with your chastity belt, Ry," Mindy quipped before turning to go.

"That lady's got some nerve," Lenny muttered as Mindy took off in a jaunty strut, no doubt to annoy Lenny even more. "If she costs you a professional relationship with an important owner like Jake Carter, Mindy will have to answer to me."

"It's okay, Lenny. You know Mindy likes to joke around. There's not a lot of females here to spar with, so she likes teasing me."

Lenny placed his muscular arms on his hips and frowned. "I don't like her talking to you so much. Or me, for that matter. That gal is trouble."

Ryder put a hand on his shoulder. "You're getting grouchy in your old age, you know. She's only having fun. I don't mind if it's at my expense." She dropped a kiss on his forehead and practically felt his mood lighten. When she let go he took off with a strut in his step.

Ryder was less happy. She had winced at Mindy's words. Was her friend right? It had been quite a while since she'd had a date, but that didn't mean she wore a chastity belt. Did it? She'd gone out with Pete a year or two ago. That counted, right? Not that there had been more than a handful of dates. Pete was a nice enough guy, but when he needed too much of her time she had bolted. The only thing that mattered was getting herself established as a horse trainer. To finally be a success at *something*.

Her thoughts were interrupted by a purposeful cough from a little man with light brown skin and dark brown eyes. His brown hair was cropped tight to his head, a mere whisper of a crown. From his diminutive stature, Ryder guessed he was a jockey. Currently dressed in denim, the man no doubt felt more at home wearing racing silks. "Excuse me, I'm here to see Ryder Hannon. Do you know where she is?"

There was a faint trace of Spanish accent in his voice. It made his words melodious.

"I'm Ryder Hannon." She turned her head and called out, "Lenny!"

The old man was back in an instant. He folded his arms across his chest and raked his eyes over the newcomer to size him up.

The smaller man extended his hand. "Emanuel Velasquez."

Though he had offered the handshake to Lenny, Ryder decided to shake it herself after Lenny let it hang in the air. "Emanuel, this is Lenny Godfried. He helps me run everything around here."

"Which one of you is the head trainer?" Emanuel asked.

"She is," Lenny grunted.

Emanuel nodded. "It'll be my first time working with a woman trainer."

"Get used to it," Lenny shot out.

"I'm sure we'll work together fine," Ryder assured Emanuel.

"Yeah. Sure," Emanuel said with less conviction in his voice.

"Let's meet back up at three o'clock," she said. "Mr. Carter will be back then with the horse."

"Handsome Dancer, I know. I've heard he's difficult, but I'm sure he'll be a piece of cake."

Ryder felt her forehead scrunch up. A too-confident jockey was never a good sign. But one reluctant to work with her would be worse. She blinked back the headache she felt coming on and chose her words carefully. "I hope you're right but from what I understand about Handsome Dancer we'll both have our work cut out for us. We'll need to handle him with great care."

"Sure," Emanuel quipped casually. "Not a problem."

Ryder closed her eyes and hoped she didn't visibly wince again.

It was a relief to have Lenny clear his throat. "Ms. Hannon will let you know what is, and isn't, a problem. You are dismissed." The old man practically puffed out his chest when he spoke.

Emanuel stiffened and gave a curt nod. "I'll go meet my valet now."

"That's a good idea," Lenny responded coldly.

When Emanuel was out of sight, Lenny narrowed his eyes. "I don't like that guy."

She bit back a grin. "I can see that. I've got to admit I have my doubts about him, too. He must be a good jockey if Jake hired him, but his confidence level is troubling. Sure I want a jockey who believes he can win, but he has to be able to understand the challenge ahead. I'll give him the benefit of the doubt. For now anyway."

"You going to tell Mr. Carter your concerns?"

"Nope."

Lenny shot her a squinty-eyed look.

"Don't do that, Lenny. You know we need this business if we're ever going to expand. I'm tired of being boxed out of stalls by the bigger trainers. Just because I'm a woman doesn't mean I don't do my job well."

Lenny placed a rough, calloused hand on her bare shoulder.

She almost winced from the feel of his fingers on her sunburnt skin. *I should stop wearing tank tops if I'm going to be in the sun all day.*

But Lenny seemed to sense her reaction was emotional instead of physical. "You don't need to keep proving yourself, Ryder. Anybody who can't see your talent is a chauvinist. You can do the job." Lenny cleared his throat. "Your father would be proud."

When she bit her lower lip, he pressed her further. "Is this about you not racing anymore?"

She shook her head. "No. Not really."

Lenny crossed his arms over his chest and gave her a flat stare. "You can't live in the past. You've got to focus on the future. And trying to prove yourself to others isn't going to do that for you. Only *you* can do that for you." Lenny's gaze shifted away as a look of disgust crossed his face. "Mindy, why are you always around here? Don't you have horses to train? If not, that's too bad because we're not hiring."

A large grin spread across Mindy's tan face. Her trademark long brown braid hung over the left side of her denim shirt. "You're not? Are you sure? Because I see you had a new jockey in here this morning. I wanted to get the 4-1-1."

"You can dial 4-1-1 all you want because we're not picking up the phone," Lenny shot back. He grumbled under his breath, "If you weren't a woman, you'd be dialing 9-1-1."

"Down, boy," Mindy retorted with an even bigger grin.

"Mindy, stop teasing him. Lenny, lighten up will you?"

"Who you hang around with is your problem," he groused before walking away.

When he was gone, Ryder put her hands on her hip and gave Mindy a frown. "Why do you tease him?"

Mindy shrugged. "Why not? Anyway, what's the skinny with the new jockey?"

Ryder answered her and then relayed her concerns. As much as Lenny detested Mindy, Ryder trusted her. Getting input from another trainer could only help.

"I agree you should give Velasquez a little leeway. For now. If he doesn't snap into place you'll need to crack the whip." She grinned. "Just because you don't like whips on horses, doesn't mean you can't use one on a man."

Ryder laughed.

"In fact," Mindy added with an even wickeder grin. "Some men like it." She took the leather crop in her hand, bent toward the ground, and gave the earth a sharp *thwat*.

"You're terrible," Ryder answered, not meaning it.

"Joking aside," Mindy said after she stopped laughing, too, "I heard some of your conversation with the grumpy troll. As usual, I don't agree with him."

"Oh? On what?"

"You can't help living in the past if the past is what you want." Mindy paused, her expression soft. "Is a part of you upset with the new jockey because *you* still want to be the jockey?"

The question made Ryder's head spin so sharply it was like suffering a bout of vertigo. "No, no. Of course not. I love being a trainer. Less dangerous. Longer career. It's a much better bet."

Mindy arched an eyebrow. "Sounds like your philosophy for your lack of love life, too."

"Geez, Mindy. It's just that I don't need distractions from my goals—"

"I'm not sure you know what your goals are," Mindy interrupted.

Ryder stood there speechless. "But . . ." Her words trailed off.

Mindy arched a single eyebrow and said nothing for a minute. "I only say these things because I care. You know I'll support whatever you want to do in life, Ry. Just make sure to be true to yourself." She gave Ryder a quick hug and headed off in the direction opposite Lenny's. "See you later," she called out behind her.

Ryder stayed frozen. Mindy may mean well but she couldn't be right. Her decision to be a trainer was all about safety. Nothing more. Because horseracing was one of the most dangerous sports in the world. Life as a jockey meant understanding your mortality. As well as the mortality of the people around you. Including the ones you loved most. Like her father. The path of safety was always the best route to follow.

The physical pain from her failed race was long gone. The scars on her body, however, remained. And yet, the residual mental pain she dragged around like oversized suitcases was the worst baggage of all.

She tried to stay optimistic. Moved on with life as best she could. Living life with both feet planted firmly on the ground. Her journey moving forward started when she earned her trainer's license from the State of New York. Then getting involved in a solid business. One she was successfully growing. Yet still she'd always wonder.

"Bye, Mindy," Ryder said softly. She didn't know why, her friend had already gone.

Lenny and Mindy both wanted what was best for her. That much was clear. But they advocated opposite things. Lenny wanted her safe. Mindy wanted her to put herself out there. To gamble. To take a chance on a dream.

If only I knew the answer myself.

When Jake stopped by at three o'clock with Handsome Dancer in tow he practically spun with nervous energy.

Nervous as to how the training would go, sure. But also pleased to be seeing her. The woman was beautiful, brilliant with horses and obviously kind hearted. He had the feeling, though, that there were many layers buried under there. Layers he wanted to unearth.

How Ryder had had this effect on him, and so quickly, he had no idea. Normally, he was the one who kept a safe emotional distance from women. Especially after his engagement to Betsy had tanked faster than a ruptured water tower. The pain to his heart, and his wallet, was taking a hell of a long time to heal. Nothing was worse than being used.

Horses were a surer bet than women. Less emotional baggage. And they listened and did what you told them. Except, of course, Handsome Dancer. But with any luck, even this wild horse could be tamed. And thrive.

Sometimes, though, luck passed him by. A year ago, Jake had bought a filly named Sky Bound, the horse Betsy had wanted. Only to then have her dump him when he became financially overstretched from the expense. He had never wanted that loser horse in the first place. Investments made with the heart and not the head were dangerous risks. *I should have stuck to my gut. I'd be a lot richer.*

Focusing on Handsome's success, as well as Jake's overall success, was critical. Because the last time he wooed a woman he made a terrible bet. Business was the better move. The risks were quantifiable and calculable. The downside—being bored to tears from the dryness of it all—was easily fixed by watching the races. The thrill of a big win, with all the prestige that went with it, easily provided sufficient highs to make life worth living.

He could only hope his gut with Handsome Dancer was equally correct. Handsome had to win. Jake might be a chump when it came to females and fillies, but not when it came to colts and stallions. Which was why he was so focused on getting the right trainer. Even if it meant cashing in a few favors to get an extra stall for Ryder. His efforts were all meant for a big-payoff.

Whether the pay-off was strictly financial with her, however, he was no longer sure. Ryder had striking beauty. There was more to her, however, than being blessed physically. Her petite frame belied her strong nature. It took great guts to be a jockey, and even more guts to have attempted the field as a woman. Being a trainer was challenging, too. For a soft-spoken lady with an equally large soft spot for animals, she was certainly nobody's pushover. A far cry from the debutant types he'd been dating. Like, Betsy. The largest challenge Betsy had ever taken on was *him*. Which, in retrospect, made them both losers.

Ryder waved to him from a distance, and he dropped his unconscious grimace. She was talking to a tall young man who was hot walking a beautiful bay. After a minute, he managed to catch her eye again. With a friendly wave, she came over. Her blond bob was in a short ponytail, loose strands flying in every direction from the warm breeze. The leggings pushed into her leather boots hugged every curve in an enticing way. A sleeveless flowery top fluttered, happily giving brief glimpses of her tight midriff. Her face seemed bronzer than the day before and infinitely more relaxed. Her countenance only made her more attractive. Blue eyes shone like the sky with strong afternoon sun.

"Hi," he said, grateful to have pushed out the words. "That horse is beautiful."

"Yes," she agreed. "But who needs beauty when you've got handsomeness?" She placed her hand on his horse's nose.

The animal greeted her with an answering whinny.

"I can't wait to work with you."

"Guess he feels the same way." As if the horse understood English, Handsome Dancer brushed his big, broad head against Ryder's shoulders. "Maybe you two should get a room."

She gave an unrestrained laugh. "I told you, he's a lover not a fighter." After a moment, she sobered. "Really, there is no telling how he'll react to me once we start training him. If he's loath to be ridden as you say, I'll still have a challenge on my hands. Today I'm just going to let him get settled. Tomorrow we'll get him started, but slowly. I'll need time to figure out what makes him tick. Give me two weeks with him. Then you can stop by, and we can chat about any progress. Fair enough?"

"Of course," he answered, though not being able to see her for two weeks wasn't really fair at all. "Good luck with Handsome Dancer."

"Thanks," she answered, already distracted by the horse.

He gave her one last glance before leaving. He saw her hand wrap around Handsome's big head in a way that made him feel a pang of jealousy he didn't understand.

Chapter 4

It had only been two days since Jake saw Ryder at Belmont's stables. At this point, he was already feeling antsy. He was doing his best not to get in touch with her.

Should he call her? *No.* If he did he would be a crazy, control freak owner. Or worse, a school kid with a crush. Which would be totally unfair because he was neither. Right?

He muttered a few colorful phrases he hoped the bartender didn't hear. Country clubs had rules on etiquette, even in their bar. He chewed silently on his thoughts while waiting for Steven, his brother-in-law, to return from the bathroom.

What was it about Ryder that drew him in? Was it the way she treated Handsome Dancer? Her kindness to his horse, and all the horses in her care, went beyond mere professionalism. It bordered on motherly.

Not that motherly was the way he saw her. Not after he'd seen her in that sundress. She'd radiated that day, a siren. Maybe she was a witch.

Could be. Even a hardened, tough-minded male like Handsome Dancer had easily fallen under her power of persuasion. No fight. No lag time. Nada. Just *poof* and then right under her spell. Her immense magic taking immediate effect.

No, Ryder wasn't a horse whisperer. She was an all-living-things whisperer. Even if she wasn't a witch, there was no denying he was bewitched. *Damn, Jake. Shake it off. Women are bad news.*

"Hey lover boy, you dreaming about your new trainer? You've been talking about her all night."

Jake spun around in his chair at the bar of the country club to see Steven mock him with a falsetto voice and fluttering eyelashes. And then Steven clasped his arms together in a girly kind of way.

Then, as if that mockery was not enough, his bald, middle-aged, slightly paunchy brother-in-law crooned, "Ohhh, Jakey, you're so handsome. You know you want to kiss me."

Good thing I know he's kidding around. And married to my sister. She wouldn't be happy if I punched him out. Dina didn't believe her husband would ever dole out this kind of crap. No wonder. Steven pretended to be the innocent around his wife. It was an act easy to believe. Most people would never guess from Steven's buttoned-up conservative appearance he was a giant jokester.

Oh well, if I can't beat 'em, join 'em. "Yeah Steven, I'm dreaming all right. And now you're in my dream with me. Forget about my new trainer. You can be my lover instead." He pursed his lips together in an exaggerated pretend kiss.

Steven faked gagging. "You can love family, but you can't *loooove* family."

"Love you? I want to kill you," Jake ground out.

"Awww. Why is Jakey so moody? Girl troubles?"

Jake glanced at Steven's fifth beer with distain. "You can't possibly be drunk from beer, can you? Real men get drunk on scotch."

"Let's find out," Steven shouted, dangerously loud for the country club bar. "Hey, bartender, two scotch whiskies over here, please!"

"Steven, lower your voice, will you? You don't want the club to kick us out. And Dina will kill you if she hears you're acting up. She never lets you out of the house as it is. Keep it up, and she'll hire a guard to make sure it never happens again." He escorted Steven to a table further away from the bar, off in a corner. They each took a seat.

A moment later, the bartender set their drinks down with a courteous nod.

"What's up with you, Steven? Is Dina making you crazy? I love my sister but I know she can be . . . particular in how she handles things."

"Yeah. *Particular*. She wants another baby. I don't want a fourth child. Having three boys is more than enough."

Jake didn't know whether to laugh or grimace at the news. "Uh, maybe your sex lives is something I ought to stay out of . . ."

"It's not only about the sex, Jake. It's how she acts. Dina wants to treat me like a stud. Like one of your horses. Shoved into a breeding barn with a filly in heat and forced to have a go at it."

Jake tried to loosen the tie and top button of his collar. "Yeah, Steven, I'm not sure I should be hearing all this . . ."

"Okay. Fine. Let's focus on you. Tell me about the hot fox you've got a thing for. Don't lie, because I've known you for fifteen years now, so I'll know if you do."

Jake sputtered. "All right. You've got me. Maybe I do have a *thing,* as you put it, for the trainer I recently hired. She's . . ." His voice trailed off as he played with the small wet napkin under his glass. *I'm going to sound like an idiot.* "She's nice. That's all."

He watched Steven put down the shot of whiskey and release a howl of drunken laughter. "*Nice*? You mean her body's nice, don't you?"

Jake's punching arm got twitchy again. "Stop pretending you're an ass, will you? You treat Dina great. I know you respect women."

"Yeah, okay, I do." Steven hung his head low. "You're killing my image. Killing it!" he yelled at the top of his lungs.

Jake winced as the bartender shot them a stern look.

"Whoa, bro," Jake admonished. "You've got to keep it down."

Steven's voice began to quiver. "I love my wife."

"I know you do. But keep it down, will you?"

"How 'bout you?" Steven asked in a dramatic whisper. "You want a wife?"

Jake raked a hand roughly through his hair. "You know you're slurring your words, right?"

"Noth I'mph not!"

"Yes, you are. I'll be driving you home for sure."

"Ansther my question. Do you wanna wifey or what?"

"Are you offering one?" Jake answered dryly.

"No." Somehow Steven managed a smile through his alcoholic haze.

Jake smiled back. Steven was a nut but he was funny, and family. "Yeah, man. I want to get married." Jake shut up at the sudden tug of his heart. "I thought I had the real thing with Betsy. It'd be nice to have more than business partners to talk to. A life partner, you know? I see what you and Dina have, and I think it's pretty great."

Steven's face lit up. "You need a girlfriend." Then his face turned into a scowl. "Dina's been hounding me to set you up. She has one of my cousins in mind."

"Forget it. Nothin' doin'." Jake called over the bartender. "Can I get another whiskey double?" As soon as the drink was placed in front of him he drained the glass. Seconds later, he waved to the bartender again and ordered one more. *Guess we'll both be taking a cab home.*

"Another beer, here!" Steven shouted at the top of his lungs.

Jake grimaced. The amount of the tip he'd have to leave the poor beleaguered bartender would be staggering.

When they finished their drinks they picked up their conversation. "Anyway, you're right about not wanting to be fixed up," Steven slurred. "My cousin Maude is a real troll."

Jake couldn't help it, he laughed. "Not nice, Steven."

"All right, that was too harsh. Maude looks like an anteater. Really long nose and very round body."

"*That* was nice?"

"To anteaters? Probably not. How about bagpipes then? Bagpipes have long skinny protrusions with a great big baggy gut. Just like Maude."

"Wow, Steven. You make a great pitch for dating her. If your successful real estate business ever fails you can always start a dating website. Call it *bagpipebellychicks.com*. I'm sure you'll gets lots of hits."

Steven leaned forward over the tiny table, his eyes wide. "Do you really think so, Jakey?"

"Nope. Not even a hard-up Scotsman would log on."

"Damn. Dina wanted me to earn more money. She's thinking of having an extension built onto our house."

Jake frowned. "It's already got six bedrooms. How much bigger does she need?"

"She doesn't. But you know how it is, always keeping up with the Joneses. Maryellen Butler and Lydia Knightly are building additions so now Dina feels she needs to do this, too. And you know how your father is, always wanting us to showcase a lifestyle suitable for the—" Steven made air quotes. "—rich and famous." He gave a loud belch and then continued, his voice shaky. "But I don't wanna pay for it. The real estate market has been dicey." Steven then twisted his body around to the bar and called over for another beer.

The bartender gave them a stern look. "I already let the concierge know you guys either need to be picked up by somebody or have a car service called," the elderly gentleman said. The tone wasn't rude but it left no opportunity for rebuttal.

"We figured. It's not a problem," Jake answered, now free to slur his words, too. Seconds later, their drinks appeared.

Steven picked his glass up with apparent delight and took a sip. "Dina told me your dad wants you to date, too."

"Are you still blathering on about my love life?"

"You mean your *lack* of love life."

Jake exhaled a hard breath of air that sounded like a hiss. "You're worse than either of them."

"Nope. They're way worse."

"Worse on multiple levels. My dad wants me to date only who he wants me to date. Society types. How do you think I got hooked up with Betsy?"

"Oh. That would explain it."

"You didn't like her either."

Steven took another swig. "Not a bit."

Jake laughed. "I wish I could say the same. To this day I'm amazed I actually fell for someone like her."

"Fell for her, huh?" Steven started to sing "Timber" in a falsetto voice that would insult both Pitbull and Kesha.

Jake gave him a flat stare. "Lucky for you I'll attribute all this to the alcohol."

Steven sucked down a third of the glass in one gulp. Another audible burp followed. "Sorry. But's not my fault I'm drunk. *You* got me drunk," he pretended to accuse.

"Yeah, right. I think you got *me* drunk."

"No way, bro." Steven's phone rang. "'scuse me. It's the wifey. I'd better take her call, if I know what's good for me." He muttered under his breath, "She's almost as scary as your father."

"Duh. No shit, Sherlock." Jake nodded until a feeling of vertigo hit him. "Double shit." *Definitely had too much to drink.* Five minutes later, Steven was still talking on the phone. Well, more like listening, since his mouth was closed, his head hung in shame. Whatever bashing Dina was dolling out, Steven was taking it. It was amazing the amount of crap a guy would take if he loved a woman.

Jake glanced at his own smart phone, which lay on the little table, silent. It would be nice if his phone rang with a woman on the other end. Double bonus points if the woman was not ranting. Or his sister. Or his ranting sister. He shuddered.

Unconsciously his fingers glided over the phone's icons as if trying to find out on their own who to contact. Until the bartender distracted him, putting some pretzels and chips down in front of him. When Jake thanked him, and the bartender had left, he heard his phone miraculously ringing. *What the . . . ?*

"Hello?" said a feminine voice he could not forget.

Shit.

"Hello, Jake? Are you there? I think you just called me. Are you worried about Handsome Dancer?"

His skin twitched from wincing. "Sorry, Ryder. I didn't mean to call you. My mistake."

Melodious laughter rang through the air. "You butt-dialed me? At eleven o'clock at night? Good to know you're still active at this hour. *I* was fast asleep. I wake up early to take care of horses, you know. Like yours, for instance."

Thank God she sounds amused.

"Jake, you are there, aren't you?"

"Yes. Yes, I'm here." He gulped loudly then winced again, hoping his phone didn't transmit the sound.

"Are you okay?"

"Yes. A little drunk is all."

"Where are you? Are you by yourself? Do you need a ride?"

"No. The country club already arranged car service for us." He heard nothing. Silence. "Ryder? Are you still there?"

"Yes, of course." Her voice sounded tighter now. "I hope you and your date get home safe."

"Date?" His voice sounded impassioned now, even to his own ears. "Who said anything about a date?"

"You said *us*. So I thought, well, never mind. As long as you've got someone to watch out for you I won't have to worry."

But I don't have someone to watch out for me. That's why *I worry.*

"Good night, Jake. Take care."

"Wait!"

"I'm sorry, what?"

"I said—I said *wait*. I'm sorry I dialed you by accident. But I'm not sorry we're talking."

An exasperated exhale came through the phone line. "Go back to the person you're with, Jake Carter. And sober up."

"You can tell I'm really drunk, huh?"

"I'd have to be deaf to not figure it out. Go back to the person you're with and go home."

He paused. Maybe because she knew he was drunk he could get away with his next words. "I'd rather talk to you. Have you bring me home. I like you, Ryder Hannon. I like you a lot."

She laughed. "You had more to drink than I thought. Are you sure your country club is calling car service for you?"

"I may be drunk but I'm also honest. I think you're hot." His head was swimming. He hoped to God he wouldn't regret this in the morning.

"Okay, Romeo. I'll be nice and forget all about this little drunk dialing escapade. Have a good ni—"

"I'm serious, Ryder. It's not the alcohol talking. I'm attracted to you. You're so kind. To everybody, not just animals. It's like you have magical charms and everything falls under your spell. *I'm* under your spell."

"Jake—"

"I'm serious! I think you're amazing. Beautiful inside and out."

She was quiet. His heart beat fast and heavily. "Say something, Ryder. Anything. We can always deny later this phone call ever happened. No matter what, I still want you training Handsome Dancer."

After a moment, her voice came through the line, no louder than a whisper. "Promise we'll forget this conversation ever happened?"

His heart was now thundering in his chest. "I give you my word."

"I like you, too, Jake."

Her voice was so soft. Had he heard wrong? Or maybe she just meant she liked him as an owner. Or a friend.

"Have a good night, Jake."

"You, too, Ryder."

"Thanks," she said quietly before hanging up.

Jake felt a hole in his stomach. Nerves from talking to her? Or alcohol-induced nausea? He was starting to feel lightheaded, too. Given the fact his brother-in-law's face was bloated and green, Steven was faring no better.

"I've got to go," Steven said miserably. His head hung low like a hound dog that'd been punished for behaving badly.

"Right. Let me get a paper bag before I get into a car with you."

"Me? You're no better. You look like you're gonna puke, too."

"No way. I'm made of steel."

The two men left the bar, passing several lushly decorated corridors before they reached the front lobby of the grandiose facility. The concierge came right over to them. "We have car service already waiting for you two gentlemen."

"Thanks. And thank the bartender for me, will you?"

"Yes, of course, sir. But a woman called us about your need for car service, too."

Steven was miserable again, his eyes downcast like a defeated dog. "Damn. Dina doesn't trust me. I told her we'd make sure we got home safely."

"Sorry to correct you, sir, but the lady who called was a Ms. Hannon."

A large grin spread out over Jake's face. "I guess she does care," he marveled.

"Yeah," Steven said, elbowing Jake in the gut. "It's awesome to be cared about, don't you think?"

"Yes, I do," Jake agreed, meaning it.

Chapter 5

When Ryder showed up to the stables the next day, it wasn't a surprise to see Mindy waiting for her with her usual Cheshire cat smile. What was unusual was the fact that Mindy wasn't there to spill the details about a night of debauchery. No, Mindy's purpose was to get Ryder to spill the details of her evening.

"Mindy, are you stalking me or something?" Ryder half-teased. How would you know if I was speaking to Jake Carter late last night?"

"I have my ways." Mindy smiled mysteriously. When Ryder crossed her arms over her chest and arched an eyebrow, Mindy expelled a loud huff of air. "Oh all right, I'll 'fess up. My friend Chuck was filling in for the regular concierge at the country club."

"The same Chuck you always talk about? The one you want to hook up with?"

"Yep. I must mention you a lot to him, too, since he recognized your name." A slow smile spread across her face. "And he also recognized Jake Carter's name. So spill."

"There's nothing much to say."

Mindy frowned. "Are you going to give me that? Seriously?"

Ryder sighed. "Yeesh, all right. But there really isn't that much to it. Jake butt-dialed me and since I could tell he was drunk I called the country club to make sure he had a ride."

"He butt-dialed you? Why can't I ever get that lucky?" She pretended to sigh dramatically. "I wish Jake Carter would butt-dial me. He's *sooooo* dreamy!"

Ryder bit back a laugh. "Are you done?"

"Hardly."

"What is it you want to know exactly?"

"Do you two have the hots for each other, or what?"

Ryder bit her lower lip. "I like him," she said cautiously. "For an owner he's extremely open to listening to what a trainer has to say."

"That's not what I meant, and you know it," Mindy chastised. "I've known you a long time. You're not dead. Why do you act it? Are you allergic to romance or something? Jake is mega hot, huge in this industry, and seems to really be into you."

Ryder took in Mindy's words but didn't answer.

"Come on, Ryder," Mindy urged. "Love is like horseracing. They're both gambles. But they're risks worth taking."

"What makes you think Jake is ready to gamble on love? He only butt-dialed me, for God's sakes. You make it sound like he proposed."

"I'd take a proposition from him any day."

"Mindy, cut it out, will you? I said *proposed* not *propositioned.*"

Mindy laughed. "Start with one to get to the other."

Ryder shot her a look.

"Okay, okay," Mindy relented. "I'm being serious now. You want to blow off the significance of his phone call as a mere butt-dial. Let's see. Did Jake hang up once you answered? Or did he want to talk to you instead?"

"Talk to me, of course, but it would have been rude otherwise."

"He could have simply apologized and hung up."

"He tried."

"Not hard enough apparently. It wouldn't have been rude to end the call. Mistakes happen. But he talked to you for a while, didn't he?" When Ryder bit her bottom lip and stayed silent Mindy pressed more. "What did he say?"

Ryder shook her head.

"Spill," Mindy insisted.

"He said I'm amazing," Ryder said so softly it was hard to even hear herself.

"Amazing, huh?" Mindy's grin was bigger than Texas. "I don't think he butt-dialed you at all. I bet it was an excuse to talk to you."

"Mindy, you're being crazy as—"

"Sure I'm crazy," Mindy interrupted with a wave. "But I'm not blind. When I saw him stare at you the last time he was here, it was with eyes so hot I'm surprised they didn't leave scorch marks on your skin. They practically branded you, like you're a horse from the Wild West."

"You're exagger—"

"Nope. I remember it crystal clear. I wish Chuck would look at me that way." Mindy lowered her volume. "I wish anyone would look at me that way. I'd be all over that. He wouldn't have to look like Jake Carter or even have powerful connections. Or gobs of money. I'd simply be happy if the guy's into me. Truly into me." Mindy contorted her face. "I'm thirty-eight years old, Ryder. I'm physically fit, but nowhere near your petite size. I don't have your blue eyes or your blond hair. My long brown braid already has some grays in it . . ."

Ryder leaned forward and wrapped Mindy in her arms. "You are young. You are beautiful. You are vibrant. And have your whole life ahead of you. You will find a fabulous man to see in you all the wonderful things I do."

Mindy gave a hard sniff when Ryder let her go. "Thanks, Ry. I needed to hear that. Despite all my teasing, I have a soft side that's *waaaaay* too soft." She let out a small laugh. "What about you, though? Are you ever going to take a chance?"

"I take chances," Ryder protested.

Mindy crossed her hands over her chest, mimicking Ryder.

"Funny," Ryder said tightly. "Ha ha ha, you're acting like me."

"I'm not trying to be funny," Mindy said. "You helped me so I'm trying to help you. Whether you want my help or not. You don't take chances. Not since you fell off—"

"Don't go there," Ryder warned.

"And why not?" Mindy demanded. "It's true. You don't want to take a chance because you don't want to fail again. I know you want to be a jockey, but it's safer to sit on the sidelines, training. I know you want Jake Carter, but again, rather than go for it and put yourself out there where you can be hurt, you sit on the sidelines taking the safe route in life."

Ryder felt her eyes go wide, her jaw hang open.

"It's true," Mindy said gently. "Take a risk in life, Ry. You have faith in me. You want me to be happy. I feel the same about you." She leaned forward and wrapped her arms around her, giving Ryder a kiss on the cheek before turning to go.

"Love ya," Mindy called out as she left the stalls behind.

Ryder watched her go. Was Mindy right? Was it time to take a chance? To get back in the saddle again?

No. Right now she was still suffering from too many scars. Emotionally and physically. Would she ever be able to bare that part of herself to him?

Chapter 6

Jake returned to Ryder's stable a week and a half later, not believing the scene unfurled in front of him. *Is that a goat? And a bunch of chickens?* He felt his forehead wrinkle. This was supposed to be a professional establishment, not a barn for rundown broncos. He was readying himself to barge in to her office and demand an explanation for her rendition of *Little Stable on the Prairie* when Ryder came up to him. Her white teeth gleamed in a wide-open smile.

Batting her hands against her jeans, a cloud of dust rose up. He coughed. "Sorry," she apologized.

Even dirty she was a jewel. Dirt never bothered him although Betsy would have killed herself. Betsy saw dirt as working class. He merely saw it as indicative of hard work. And hard work was an enviable trait to find in someone. It was something he was glad to have in common with the beautiful, albeit dirty, woman in front of him. At least her smile was bright, her pearly white teeth were as beautiful as the rest of her.

"Hope my appearance doesn't scare you away," she apologized. "Barn work is real dirty and we needed to make some changes around here, as you can see." She gestured around at the cacophony coming from the loose chickens. A loud, annoyed, *"meh!"* brought his attention to the mangy goat standing off to the side.

Goat pellets littered the floor of her horse stalls, along with loose feathers. One small white wisp drifted past his face. He blew it away with a hard exhale. But the feather blew back and stuck against his lower lip. His lip twitched as he hastily brushed it off.

"There's more," she said with obvious pride. "I installed a beach ball on a tether in his stall. He can bat it around when he gets bored. So, tell me, do you like what we've done?"

"Er, no."

"What? You've got to be kidding me! We worked so hard to do this for Handsome Dancer. And he's responded so well to everything."

"Responding well to what? Chickens?" He felt his eyebrows raise as high as his hairline. *I must be missing her logic.*

He could see her quiet down. She pushed some blond, flyaway strands behind her ears and straightened herself up. She tugged her oversized denim shirt more squarely on her shoulders, as if she was trying to look more professional and less ragged, putting a lid on a temper about to explode. And then her eyes clouded like an incoming storm.

Uh-oh. I guess I did miss something. Something about her, anyway. She's got a volcano hidden inside her.

"Yes. Chickens. And Clem, the goat standing over there."

"I don't get it. What's up?" he asked.

"Handsome Dancer needed animal friends. Clearly he wasn't taking to humans too well if he kept throwing them off. I picked a goat and some chickens because they can roam free. Some horses feel very lonely when they're left all alone in stall. They can't even see the horse next to them. It's isolating."

"I thought Handsome Dancer hated being around anything. That's why he couldn't be ridden."

"I think he was having trouble being broken because his heart's broken. I mean, if you had no friends, wouldn't you be in a bad mood?"

"I guess so."

"Same for your horse. It's an old tactic, actually. Ever hear the phrase, 'to get someone's goat'? It originated from unscrupulous horse owners stealing another racehorse's pet goat. The racehorse would get very upset and then lose the race. All I did was to employ the reverse trick. Giving a horse a pet goat so he'd win his races." Ryder's face beamed with pride at her ingenuity.

She's pretty clever. Or pretty crazy.

"I gave Handsome Dancer friends. Friends he can see because they can come to his stall. This way Handsome and his friends can communicate.

Jake felt his eyebrow arch up. "Dr. Doolittle, I presume?"

A slow smile spread across her lips.

"How far have you gotten with Handsome?"

"He'll let me ride him now."

Jake's eyebrows shot up to his hairline. "My God, Ryder, you're amazing," he exclaimed. With a shake of his head and a hard cough he corrected himself. "I mean, your results with him are amazing."

Ryder's grin was now Cheshire cat sized. "Thanks for both compliments."

Damn. She couldn't let my mistake go.

Then it hit him. His comment was a slip, but was it really a mistake? Her beautiful face, which had been beaming with pride now had a shy aspect that was even more endearing. She bore a schoolgirl's blush and averted her eyes from him as she busied herself petting Handsome's nose.

If only she could stroke me the same way. Though somewhere lower down than my nose. He tensed at the thought. *Focus, Jake, damn it! This is business.* "Show me," he said.

She blinked. "Show you what?"

"Show me Handsome Dancer can be ridden. I want you to ride him for me."

"Now? He's already had his exercise for today. I don't want to tire him out."

Handsome's head batted her shoulder with a determination that was comical.

"You know," Jake quipped, "if he actually understands you then you really are Dr. Doolittle."

"I'm sure he just wanted me to give him an apple." She wiped a stray blond bang from her hot forehead and looked the horse in one of his eyes. "What are you saying, babycakes? That you want to go on a short ride with me?"

Yes, yes, I do. Jake cleared his throat and gave her a tight smile. "Go ahead, you two. Impress me."

A few minutes later, he was outside the training track, his hands casually resting on the guardrail while he waited for the show to begin.

Soon, Ryder and Handsome entered the track. He heard her cluck her tongue at the horse, and then watched her lightly kick Handsome's rear. The horse took off around the track in a fast gallop. The horse's flight was fluid and astoundingly fast for what was supposed to be an easy go-around. She was doing more than merely riding Handsome Dancer. She was a part of him. One cohesive whole.

Thinking the demo was about to end, he had almost turned around to head back when something caught the corner of his eye. It was a flash of color, a fast burst of brown. *What the . . . ?* Whipping his head around to the source, he stared open-mouthed at the sight. Handsome Dancer was bolting down a stretch of training track at a speed unheard of for a newbie horse. Or maybe any horse. In all of Jake's experiences, he doubted he had seen a horse move that fast when not performing in an actual race.

As impressed as he was, he frowned. Was Ryder working Handsome too hard? Tiring a horse out with a training exercise was a bad idea all around. Both emotionally and physically for the horse. As someone who cared about his animals' well-being, the potential emotional impact was something important to worry about. Stressing out a horse by constantly spurring it on could lead to depression. The risk of negative physical impact was no better. And likely a whole lot worse. Pulled tendons or muscles could leave the horse permanently lame, which could impact the horse's psychological state, too.

How sure was he Ryder knew what she was doing? By the time she dismounted, handing Handsome over to a hot walker after affectionately kissing his sweaty, heavily breathing nose, he was more than ready to find out. He straightened himself up to his full height and peered down at the smiling face. Her rail-thin body was over a foot shorter than his but her obvious pride in her accomplishment seemed to puff her up until she loomed as large as him.

"Well? Whadja think?" she demanded. Her grin had grown even larger. If she beamed any brighter she'd pass as a lighthouse.

His lips twisted around until he formed his carefully chosen words. "I'm glad to see you got him to perform."

Her smile dropped, a heavy rock tossed off the lighthouse's cliff. "You're not happy?"

"I'm . . . I'm not sure how you got so far so fast. I don't want him pushed past his limits. To be performing this hard, to be running at that pace for a simple demo . . ."

"I am not pushing him past his limits. This is not the Belmont Stakes where everything is on the line. Handsome Dancer was merely trying to prove to you he can do it. *He* wants to show off, not me." She folded her arms across her chest and blew a stray strand of blond hair from her eyes. She didn't seem like she was challenging him as much as she was wary of him. "It's going to be hard to work for you if you're going to doubt my integrity. I break down a horse's barriers to success. But I don't break their spirit. And I would never overexert an animal just to impress an owner."

He expelled a hard breath. "Okay. I didn't think so. But if you didn't push him to the max, how was he able to take off like that? He flew around the track."

"Like you said yourself, your horse is special."

"The trainer has a lot to do with it," said a deep voice out of nowhere. The person sounded highly annoyed. When Jake turned to see Lenny's face, he knew he had called it right. Notwithstanding, Jake extended his hand and plastered on a pleasant face.

"It's okay, Lenny," Ryder said gently. "I can fight my own battles."

Her voice had the duality of light chastisement and heavy affection. She put a hand on the older man's shoulder.

A thought struck Jake. Ryder and Lenny had a father/daughter relationship. "I'm not attacking anyone," Jake explained, putting his rejected hand down.

"Good. Because Ryder here is the best. She's been doing wonders for Handsome Dancer, and if you think she'd push an animal before its ready, and for the sole reason of showing off, you don't know her at all."

"Lenny. I—" Ryder tried to cut in.

"I'm an owner." Jake straightened. "Don't you think I have the right to ask what's being done with my horse?"

Lenny's chin rose up a notch. "If you have so many doubts that you need to ask her to explain herself maybe you should—"

Ryder took a step in front of Lenny. "None of us need be hasty. Mr. Carter has a right to ask."

Jake winced. The return to formality was painful.

The old man was glaring hard at her too.

"And Lenny has a right to make sure our philosophy and technique is respected by the owners of the horses we train," Ryder hastily finished.

Her words seemed to calm Lenny down. His eyes looked less like weapons of mass destruction.

"You should appreciate all she's been doing," Lenny ground out, obviously still irritated with him. "She's been working night and day with Handsome Dancer. Had to hire another hand to make up for her lost time on the other horses she's working with so they don't suffer for it. You can see your horse is responding well to her. He's got pure power, yeah. But it's Ryder he wants to do well for. The only one trying to show off around here is Handsome Dancer. There's no doubt in my mind your horse wants her proud of him. That dang boy practically coos like a baby every time she walks by. And you ought to thank her for that."

Lenny abruptly turned and left. Ryder shot Jake a sympathetic smile before taking off after Lenny. The old man slowed down only long enough to stop for a kiss on his cheek from her and then resumed his pace back to wherever it was he was going.

Moments later, Ryder was back in front of Jake. "Sorry for that, but I'm sure you understand. You two are a lot alike."

Jake arched an eyebrow. "Really? I'm a hot-under-the-collar curmudgeon?"

Ryder bit back a smile. "I hadn't thought of that. I meant you're both highly protective of what you care most about. Lenny's protective of me. You're protective of Handsome Dancer."

He froze over the truism of her words. No wonder she did such amazing things with horses, she could read all animals—from equines to mankind. And with spot-on honesty. As if the curtains were pulled back and the stage cleared off for the person to be thoroughly revealed. She seemed to understand everybody and everything's dynamics, why reactions were what they were. Even better, she knew what to do about it, as if she reacted not to words or attitude problems, but to their real issues. And then had the ability to calm their fears and anxieties—if by doing nothing more than simply reassuring them she was there for them.

A second thought hit him. At least Lenny had someone special at the center of his life. All Jake had was his business. *Lenny is no doubt smarter than I am.* It was time to put a person at the center of his life, too. And like Lenny, maybe it was Ryder who should be in that center.

"Would you like to go out to dinner with me?" Jake blurted.

"What?" Her eyes went wide. "You feel we need to go someplace private to talk about business?"

He slipped his fingers inside his shirt collar and gave a little tug. "No, I'm asking you to go out on a date."

"You were serious when you butt-dialed me?"

He took a deep breath. *In for a penny, in for a pound.* "Serious about finding you attractive? Yes." His face felt hot.

"Hmmm. I don't know. First you seemed worried by how I train your horse, and now you're worried whether I'm willing to train you?" She laughed. The sound of it was earthy and delightful.

"Yeah. That's about right." He grinned.

"Some beasts are untrainable. Are you one of them?"

"Come find out. I never should have doubted you. I'm sorry. Let me make it up to you by taking you out to dinner. Somewhere nice. We won't talk business. Not one drop. I swear."

Ryder bit her lip, and then broke out into a smile. "Okay. We can go tonight. But just out to dinner, okay? I have work very early in the morning."

He crossed his fingers and held them over his chest. "Scout's honor. I'll see you at six. Dress nice."

Dumbfounded by the whole chain of events, Ryder wasn't sure what to make of Jake Carter but couldn't resist finding out. Lost in thought, she surveyed her dirty denim and slopped-up riding boots. Blond flyaway wisps circled around her head like an electrified halo. She batted them away with a grimy hand. *To say I look like a disaster would be an insult to disasters. A mudslide would be more attractive.*

She cringed. *Crazy he'd ask me out when I'm such a mess.* She peered down at her nails and examined the dirt in them. *No wonder he told me to look nice. Yeesh.*

Out of the corner of her eye, Mindy appeared. Ryder let out a loud "oh" of surprise.

"Hi ya," Mindy greeted.

"Good Lord, Mindy. Stop sneaking up on me. You're going to give me a heart attack."

"You don't mind when Lenny does it," Mindy retorted. "Anyway, I didn't stop by to give you a heart attack. I came by to give you a present."

Ryder felt her face light up. "Really? That's so nice of you. Really great. But it's not my birthday."

"Doesn't matter. Sometimes you need perfect timing for the perfect gift."

"Perfect timing for what?" Ryder felt her face scrunch up in confusion.

"I saw Mr. Gorgeous leave here. I'm guessing the time you'll need this will be coming up real soon."

"What will be soon?" Ryder asked, still confused.

"Take this and you'll see." Mindy tossed Ryder a small package wrapped up in colorful giftwrap. A purple bow was tied around it. "Don't wait too long to open it," Mindy called out before she disappeared.

"Heck no," Ryder chirped cheerfully. Tearing the package open, she groaned. "Mindy! You didn't!" she called out. *No wonder she took off.*

Ryder didn't have much time to contemplate the package before Emanuel approached her. She tossed the box into a stall and prayed he didn't notice her move.

"I saw you riding Handsome Dancer," he said without preamble.

Ryder nodded and did her best to smile. There was something about Emanuel's tone that seemed accusatory although that would make no sense. She waited for him to continue. Maybe he'd shed some clarity.

"He acts like he's ready to ride," Emanuel remarked. "I want to test him out in one of tomorrow's races. I can take a small one, so the stakes won't be too much and he'll get used to me."

"Despite Handsome Dancer's awesome performance today, he's still not ready. He was only trying to show off, which is great, but he has to get used to the rigors of competing in an actual race. And doing it against other horses who also want to win. He's still not comfortable enough in the gate. I'm doing everything I can to even keep his gate card. If he has to go back to school we'll all be out more time and money."

Emanuel gave a flat stare. "He won't ever get used to it until he does it more."

Ryder crossed her arms over her chest. "I'm not shoving him into anything he's not ready for. I'll let you know when he's ready to compete."

"I'm going to tell Mr. Carter I'm not going to wait around forever. Every race that goes by costs me ten percent of the winnings."

"Assuming you'd race and win. Which you wouldn't because Handsome Dancer is not ready yet." Ryder ignored the throbbing pain by her temple. Once she was rid of Emanuel she'd take some aspirin and a short stroll around the stables to help relax.

But it might be a while before she could take a break, given the reddish tint of Emanuel's face. His cheeks were puffed up as if he were about to explode. "Are you telling me I cannot win? Are you doubting me?" His voice was high-pitched, his faint accent becoming more pronounced.

She put a hand on her forehead to soothe her throbbing skull. "I'm telling you that you cannot win with Handsome

Dancer in his current state. It doesn't matter how good of a jockey you are. The horse is not ready yet."

Emanuel started to speak, but she put up a hand to stop him. "I'm not doubting your abilities. I hope you're not doubting mine."

He hesitated before grumbling, "This is costing me money."

"You'll need to work that out with Jake."

Once he left she leaned against a cool wood wall. The temperature soothed both her body and temperament.

She closed her eyes and wondered how the morning got so bizarre. Before she met Jake Carter she had a nice steady daily routine. No temperamental jockeys. No gifts from Mindy tossed at her. Even Lenny had been less grouchy. And of course there was now the issue of getting Handsome Dancer up and ready in a reasonable amount of time. He'd need to not only be able to race, but be able to get enough races under his belt before the really big races could be tried.

She felt her eyelids twitch, a supplement to her throbbing temple. *Darn all this stress. Think calming thoughts, Ry. Only calming thoughts.*

At least meeting Jake had brought her a horse that she adored working with, and one that could potentially change her career. Her life, really, if Handsome Dancer won something huge like the Belmont Stakes. Imagine what she could do with her share of the winning purse. She'd get more stalls, train more horses, and really start to make an impact in the racing community. Respect. Prestige. Everything she could never get as a jockey herself, she could get as a trainer.

She closed her eyes. A vision of Handsome Dancer on the racetrack appeared before her. She was no longer in the stalls but in the viewing stands surrounded by thousands of fans. People in the crowd periodically screamed or went silent depending on how their horse was doing.

An excited vibe filled the air as the horses neared the turn for the last stretch. A collective hush swept over the crowd. The spectators grabbed their racing forms, sweaty and wrinkled so the print could no longer be read. Thousands of human heads turned in sync as they tracked the horses racing neck-and-neck toward the finish line. Thousands of spectators' hands went above their eyes to block the sun's rays from the spectacular view. The jockeys' colorful silks reflected rays of light.

In her mind, Ryder squinted to make out which horse was Handsome Dancer. Finally, Jake's horse made its way through the throngs of charging thoroughbreds. Handsome wove in-between bigger horses on the inside, and several stocky contenders on the outside. Yes, it was Handsome Dancer coming around, in clear view for all the world to see. He was going for it, his neck stretched out as his jockey hand-rode him, as they drove themselves forward as if swept by a hurricane. They charged forward like a wind gust and passed the finish line. A full length ahead of the pack.

Moments later, Handsome took his place in the winner's circle in front of an adoring, screaming crowd. Ryder rushed forward to see him, to touch the horse that changed her world.

And when her eyes looked up at the jockey who won it all, familiar eyes stared back at her. Her own. *What the f—*

Ryder, startled by her own daydream, knocked over some tack hung up on a peg next to her on the stable wall. *Oh my God, I still want to ride.*

Hastily she picked up the fallen tack and hustled out of the stable to get some coffee and fresh air. And then she did her best to push that daydream out of her mind. Never to be thought of again.

Chapter 7

Ryder tucked a wayward strand of her blond bob behind an ear with more force than necessary. Standing around by herself in a restaurant lobby, no matter how exquisite the restaurant, was awkward to say the least. It never paid to be early. It gave too much time for doubt to creep up. Was she going to be stood up? Even if she wasn't, her date probably wasn't too anxious to see her. Ryder unconsciously rubbed an imaginary "L" off her forehead and grimaced.

At least I'm waiting around in one of the best places. Chez Louis XIV was well known to all but patronized only by those with a very big wallet. And attitude.

Standing around in high heels was no easy feat. Nor easy on the feet. But her preferred dress shoes, ballet flats, simply would not have cut it. This was not a simple, nice night out with her mom or Mindy. This was an honest-to-God legitimate date. Right? At least it would be if he ever showed up. So with that idea in mind she had donned her highest heels, four-inch platform gold and white dress sandals. Unfortunately, the braiding of the gold ropes chafed. But at least her figure would appear willowy thanks to her new height. It wasn't as if men generally clamored for a woman who stood barely over five feet tall. Even with her platform shoes on, Jake would be roughly a foot taller than her.

Instead of a tall, beautiful princess she had grown up feeling like she was the ugly dwarf. *Can I help it if short genes run in my family? Without it, Dad never would have become a legendary jockey.*

Her eyebrows knit together at the memory of the vivid daydream from earlier in the day, the one where she became a jockey again. Her tiny frame sitting tall in the saddle as she rode toward victory.

She frowned and shook the idea out of her head. Nobody, especially a rich businessman like Jake Carter, would want to be on a date with a daydreamer. Spaced out in her own world. *Geez*, even she didn't want to be around herself when she was like that. She bent down to grab her heavy gold purse off the floor to go kill time in the ladies' room, but out the corner of her eye, she caught a glimpse of a tall, handsome man. Her full attention immediately turned to the source. Jake Carter gave her a slow, sly smile.

Jake took in the sight of Ryder's sleeveless dress and smiled. Though the garment was not outright sexy, it showed off the muscular contours on her arms. Her biceps were obviously well developed and very tan. Both effects no doubt created by all her physical work with horses. Yet despite the outfit showing her strength, it showed her femininity, too. The white and gold dress hung around her gracefully like a Grecian tunic that was cinched at the waist. She was a beautiful statue, thin and surprisingly tall. He suppressed a smile when he saw her platform heels peek out from under the long dress.

She's still so tiny. In fact, her petite figure was the exact opposite of her large personality. The stark contrast was appealing. But in some ways she was internally consistent. *Strong body, strong mind.*

"You look lovely," Jake murmured.

"Thank you for the compliment," she answered softly. Her blue eyes were bright and playful. She beamed a smile.

"I hope you weren't waiting long." He glanced at his Rolex.

"I have a little bit of a time problem. I always arrive early."

He shot her a grin. "Like your horses, I hope. I love it when they arrive early, too. First to the finish line." He noted a small wrinkle spring up between her eyebrows. "Sorry. Didn't mean to talk shop."

"It's okay. Work is hard to shut out, I know."

"Tonight I'm going to make a concerted effort. I want to talk about you."

She smiled and blushed as they followed the hostess to their table. The restaurant was crowded as usual. Noisy laughter and chatter filled the air. With Ryder's soft voice he hoped her words wouldn't be drowned out. She was the only one he wanted to hear.

"Wine?" he asked when they were seated.

"No, thanks. One of us has to keep our wits."

He laughed. "I can't possibly drunk dial you again. Number one, you're right here. Number two, I'm not indulging tonight." He picked up her hand and kissed it. "Any more than being with you is already an indulgence."

"Thanks, but you don't need to pour it on so thick, you know. This is just a getting-to-know-you kind of thing."

"I'm not pouring it on. I'm being honest." He smiled, his fingers stroking hers. "Maybe it's the same thing."

"I'm not used to all this," she said, her gaze downcast. "I'm used to being all business. It takes a lot of time and attention to be a trainer."

"I'm sure it does," he answered with sincerity.

"Doubly so being a woman." She hesitated. "I know we agreed not to talk about work, but can I ask you about Emanuel?"

Given the tone of her voice, I'm sure this isn't good. "Sure. Fire away."

She gave him a timid smile. "I don't think warfare will be necessary, but I am feeling a tad defensive. He was giving me a hard time at the stables today. He was insisting he ride

Handsome Dancer in one of tomorrow's races, and I don't feel that's in the horse's best interest. Not yet anyway."

"And you felt like Emanuel was advocating for himself and not the horse? So he can get his cut of more wins?"

"I don't want to be that harsh in my assessment, but I'm not sure what else to think. Either that, or he thinks I'm a poor assessor of a horse's abilities and that I'm wasting my time, and his potential earnings, by holding out." She exhaled hard. "I shouldn't have demonstrated what Handsome's capable of on the practice track today. It gave me pride, sure, but now it's given me grief. First you were upset I was working Handsome too hard. Now I have concerns about Emanuel's performance." She twisted her mouth around. "Maybe we're all going crazy because we've never seen a horse like this before. We're all running around in circles not knowing what to do."

"Just do what you always do."

Her eyebrows furrowed. "What's that?"

"Ask the horse."

She laughed softly.

Good. I'm glad I lightened her mood. "You are Doctor Doolittle, right? Because I saw the shingle outside your office door, *Dr. Ryder Doolittle, DVM.*"

"Are you saying I should treat Handsome Dancer as a *pushmi-pullyu*?" she deadpanned.

He blinked in confusion. "It's my joke, so I should catch that line. Alas, my Dr. Doolittle knowledge has reached its end." Pretending to be sad, he shook his head.

"A pushmi-pullyu was Dr. Doolittle's llama friend in the 1960's era film. It had two heads—one faced forward and one faced its tail."

"I know a bunch of people like that. When they talk, crap comes out of their mouth."

She burst out laughing. "Hey, you said for me to talk to animals in their own tongue."

"Handsome Dancer does *not* talk crap." Jake pretended to stiffen up like he was offended. Then he gave up the ruse when the waiter came to take their orders.

"I agree Handsome is quite sincere in everything he does," she commented after the waiter left. "Including wanting to please me. I don't want to take that away from him."

"Hence your problem with Emanuel," Jake said more soberly.

"Yes. Any advice you want to give me?" Rose color rushed to her cheeks. "I can handle Emanuel on my own," she hastened to add. "But it's usually me who picks the jockeys. Since you chose him, I don't want to unduly interfere."

"I'll talk to him. In the meantime, I can pay you more money to deal with it. And him too so he doesn't feel cheated."

"But I—"

"It's already done."

"But—"

"Don't object. It's not an act of charity on my part. Money motivates people. It's a natural response. We can all stomach what we don't want if we're getting paid well for our effort." He watched her eyes open wide.

"Really? What did money ever persuade you to do that you didn't want to do?"

Crap. How'd I get myself into this situation? "There's a few things on my list."

"How'd it turn out?" She sat back in the chair and crossed her arms, waiting expectantly for an answer. "Enlighten me."

"My father is . . . outspoken on what he wants me to do. Business-wise. And personally."

She leaned forward in her chair. "Really?" she asked again. "How so?"

He chose the easiest path to follow. "I made some

investments because of him. Ones I was reluctant to make. Some worked out well. Others, not so much."

"Are you answering in the 'personal' or 'professional' category?"

"Both." He sat back in his chair and shut up. *The less said the better.*

Ryder's foot tapped rapidly up and down underneath the restaurant table's white linen cloth. She was glad for the covering so he couldn't read her body language. "Is this an actual date?" she asked softly.

His brow furrowed. "That's the general idea, yes. Otherwise, this place is an odd pick for a meal with one of my horse trainers. Last time I took a trainer out to dinner it was with Lou O'Leary. He was fine with the local diner."

"I would have been fine with that, too. I don't need anything fancy."

"Maybe not, but I'll be damned before I take one of my dates out to a local diner. Especially on a first date. Like this one, to answer your question."

"Then don't you think we ought to open up to each other? At least a little? Please?" She forced both feet flat on the floor to stop her nervous twitching. "If we stay superficial our relationship really will be strictly business." Her voice lowered further until her words were barely audible. "I want to know you more than that." Her cheeks burned. *I can't believe I'm putting myself out there. Maybe it's 'National Take-A-Risk' day.*

She waited with baited breath while the waiter put down a platter of olives, brie, and baguette in front of them. The delicious smell of garlic and olive oil from their dipping dishes filled the air.

Ryder watched his throat bob in a swallow. *Maybe he's as afraid as I am to take a risk.*

"My father has had a lot of input in my business deals. Too much. He funded a lot of them. Most of them are businesses that he technically owns but I run. He makes sure I follow along his path, and plenty of others are always happy to hop on that bandwagon." He swallowed again and paused a moment before continuing. "My father's been hugely successful all his life so there's a part of me that always felt *who am I to doubt him?*"

She nodded. "I understand what it's like to live under a father's spectacular shadow." Her hands twined together and twisted around. "It was so hard for me to create my own image. Especially as a jockey. And even more as a woman who most people wouldn't let ride anyway. It's been easier as a trainer to stake out my own turf. I've been fortunate to find some owners who at least trust me enough to do that. Like you. Thanks for believing in me, by the way. I know it's a leap of faith. As you put it, my methods are effective, but can be viewed as slightly unorthodox."

"If I didn't hire you to train Handsome Dancer I'd be sabotaging myself. One good thing I learned from having to emulate my father." Jake donned a paternalistic voice. "Never screw yourself over, son." They both laughed. "As far as training goes, I don't care if you are a woman or even another horse. As long as the job with Handsome Dancer gets done." He lowered his voice seductively. "Although it definitely helps on the personal level that you're a woman."

"Oh. You mean to say you don't date horses. Good to know," she teased.

He laughed louder. "People have accused me of being beastly, but never of bestiality. Not my thing."

She laughed, too, then shuddered. "Thank God for that."

"I'm sure you'll find me adequate in other arenas as well."

"Cocky, aren't you?" She smiled.

He raised a single eyebrow. "Now that we have the right subject matter, let me know if you care to find out. I'm sure Chez Louis XIV can be persuaded to pack our luscious French food in a doggy bag."

She glanced over at the formally dressed waiter pouring a bottle of expensive wine for a nearby patron. "I think they'd rather kill themselves than pack anything in a doggie bag."

"Remember, money talks."

"I doubt that. Once the chef hears *doggie bag* I'm sure he'll go permanently deaf from ear trauma. Or come after you with a cleaver for suggesting such a thing."

He leaned over the table, picked up her hand, and kissed it slowly. Shivers ran through her. More delicious than the expensive cheese in front of them.

"If you're willing to leave now," he crooned, "I guarantee you I will pay the chef whatever it takes. I'm begging you to dare me."

His intense gaze was making her heady. The room became a blur. The only crystal clear image was him. The rest of the world faded away.

With great effort, she pulled herself out of her trance. *This is moving all too fast. I still barely know the man on any level, let alone a personal one. Does he like me for who I am? Or for what I can do for his horse? Or worse, is he simply hoping for a good time with a one-night stand?*

"No thanks. I never take up someone's offer for a dare." She cleared her throat with a tight cough. "So, what got you interested in owning horses?"

She couldn't tell if he was amused or disappointed she changed the topic of conversation. But he did seem grateful when the waiter came over to give them their meals. "My father owns quite a few horses. I decided to go off on my own. Make my own investments. Choose my own pick of winners."

"Handsome Dancer," she acknowledged. "You mentioned there were people who were marking him up as a lost cause."

"Yes. My father being one of them." He lifted a forkful of food and left it hanging in midair. "I'm not sure if he's doubting the horse or me since I bet on the horse. He's always been like that. Second-guessing me. It takes a lot of my energy to shut him out. He's like annoying background noise."

"Elevator music a person needs to block out."

"Or go crazy. You got it. He's like the worst instrumental version of some crappy sixties' song. And I've got twenty more floors to listen to the ordeal. The tune is always the same though. *I can do it better than you.*"

"Sounds like a bad refrain."

"I wish *he'd* refrain." Jake paused to take a bite. "You mentioned your father. What about him? Did the two of you get along?"

"Very well. I was crushed when he died. He was always very supportive. He picked out my unusual name. I wish I could live up to it." She drew a circle on the linen tablecloth with her fingertip. Her eyes followed the invisible pattern, not meeting his gaze.

"You are living up to it, as a trainer." Jake narrowed his eyes as if trying to gauge her.

Her heart fluttered from the intensity of his stare. It triggered little explosions from her chest to her knees. *Keep your head together, Ry.* "I meant as a jockey." *Am I really admitting to all this? Either the man is a truth machine or he's turning me on so much I'm losing my mind.*

"Do you want to be a jockey?" There was no judgment in his voice, only sincerity.

"Oh, I want to train Handsome Dancer," she hastened to say. "I didn't mean—"

"I know you didn't. You have the job so don't worry about it. I'm talking now to Ryder the actual person, not Ryder the businesswoman. We agreed this is a date, remember?"

She nodded. "Yes. No. I don't know." She fidgeted with the tablecloth. "Good God, maybe."

"Something to think about?" he asked gently.

"I . . . I don't know. Being a jockey is so dangerous. You know I fell in my first major race. My first one as a licensed jockey. I could have been permanently injured. Or killed. And the pain I suffered wasn't just mine. The owner who took a chance on me was injured as well, albeit fiscally. And then there's this business I built up. It'd be foolhardy for me to toss it all away." Her voice trailed off.

"Isn't the horse business all about taking a gamble? Risking it all, even if the odds are against you? Trusting your gut that what you have faith in is right?"

She didn't answer him verbally. Her mind, however, was a whirlwind in its failed attempts to respond.

They finished dinner, a delicious meal she hardly tasted. Then a decadent chocolate lava desert they both shared. She didn't object when he leaned over the table to rub off a dab of chocolate from her lower lip with his thumb. She fought the urge to have her tongue jut out so she could taste him, too.

From the look on his face, the same image was playing out in his mind.

"Ready to go?" he asked rhetorically, his voice rough.

Wordlessly, she rose up from the table and took the hand Jake extended then followed him out the door. "Where to?" she asked.

"You'll know it when we get there," he said. "Leave your car. I'll send someone around to come get it. Hand the key to the hostess and it'll all be taken care of."

"But—"

He bent down to give her a hard kiss on the lips right there in the restaurant lobby. The feel of it was liquid warmth running down the length of her skin. The impact of the heat was immediate. Luckily, he'd kept his hands by his sides so she could step away before they made a scene.

"You're beautiful when you blush. You're always beautiful, actually. And I don't regret doing that."

Stunned, she blinked at him for a moment until she got her bearings. "Neither do I."

Chapter 8

Jake drove Ryder back to Belmont after dinner. She had her own living quarters, albeit temporary, in the back of the house, one of a gazillion mini apartments for the horse staff. After Jake had parked, he insisted he escort her all the way to her quarters.

The evening had been so perfect, she mused. The conversation—no, the *connection* with him—had been perfect. It had been a long time since she had opened up to anyone. Her own self included. And without offense to Lenny, sharing her innermost thoughts with the grumpy old man was not ideal. Not even if he was her actual dad.

Mindy was a good friend. The best, really, despite her teasing ways. But speaking openly to her was hard, too. It was long ago ingrained in Ryder to be tough and stand on her own. Did opening up make her seem weak?

Jake didn't make her feel that way. The more she spoke about her weaknesses the stronger she felt. She actually found it empowering, giving her a shot of self-confidence she hadn't had before, as if Jake spoke not just to her but to who she was.

Ryder was so lost in thought she barely noticed when Jake stopped walking. They were right outside a building of stalls not far from her own. New construction had recently been completed and not many horses had been housed in this new facility yet. Several sleeping mares, however, occupied spaces down at the other end.

"The evening is beautiful, isn't it?" Jake remarked offhandedly. He leaned against an outside wall, the fire in his eyes in stark contrast to the casualness of his comment.

"Yes. It's a wonder it's so warm out." Without realizing it, she closed her eyes and lifted her hands in the air. "No wind at all. And so quiet. You can hear crickets chirping."

"All I want to listen to is you."

She opened her eyes to see him watching her intently. He picked up her hand, and she relished the warmth.

"Ryder, did you have as good a time tonight as I did?"

"Yes. Everything was perfect." *Lord, you seem perfect. I hope I'm not going to fall for you.* "Thanks for taking me out to dinner."

He stroked his thumb against her hand, now held against his chest. "I need to be honest with you. I'm becoming much more interested in you than as simply a trainer for one my horses. Or even as merely one of my dates."

She watched him swallow. Somehow this simple movement was fascinating. She wanted to move forward and kiss his throat, drawn like a moth to flame.

She felt herself swallow hard too but tried to keep the conversation light. "I'm becoming more interested in you than merely my highest-paying horse owner. Or even the man with the best come-on lines."

He smiled. "Then I guess we have something in common." He put his arm around her waist but didn't take a step closer. "Is it okay if I kiss you again? If not, I promise—"

Before he could finish his sentence, Ryder's kiss cut him off. *Oh my God, I can't believe I did that. But man, the feel of his lips . . .*

Instantly, the feel of his soft skin grew hard as he held her tightly against him and crushed his lips down on hers. "Ryder," he murmured. "I've wanted to kiss you for so damn long. The one we shared back in the restaurant only made it worse. Because then I knew what I've been missing."

She pressed herself further against him. Not that there was much space left between them. The feel of his hips against hers let her know he was feeling the same intensity she was.

Until he suddenly broke away.

"What?"

"Not out in the open like this," he explained while grabbing her hand. In moments, they were inside the stalls. There wasn't a person anywhere in sight.

Ryder had never seen anything remotely romantic about horse stalls before. Not even with Mindy's endless jokes about whips and riding crops. But now the place struck her differently. The earthy smell of the clean, dirt floors. The soft whinnies of the nearby horses, woven in with the cacophony from the crickets. Even the rough feel of wood of a stall door felt rich and full of promise.

"It's so dark in here," she whispered, not wanting to disturb the slumbering horses. "I never come to the stalls at night. I should. It's so peaceful."

"Not for me," Jake quipped, taking both of her hands to his lips and kissing them. "In fact, I feel fired up. *You* fire me up. I haven't felt this engaged with someone for the longest time."

"Jake . . ." But when her mouth moved more, no words came out.

"Tell me you feel the same way, Ryder."

She managed a nod. "Yes," she finally said through the darkness.

She could feel rather than see his smile. Without a sound, he grabbed her hand and led her to an empty stall. Ryder felt soft earth beneath her feet. There was no hay to step on, the stall had not even been used. The wood stable walls felt warm. But still so much cooler than the burning feeling from her own skin.

Jake gently pushed her back against the wall. They were standing together now, his body pressed against hers.

"Maybe we should go back to my apartment," she suggested, her voice throaty.

"Not a chance." He kissed her lips softly. Then trailed kisses down her long throat. She felt her breathing speed up. Her chest almost hurt from its fast rise and fall.

"Are your clothes restricting you, too?" He laughed. His hands were upon her, opening the top buttons of her dress one by one. His fingers touched and teased her. Until they trailed her lace bra. The effect was immediate. Her nipples hardened and her breath became shallower.

"I don't think you need to wear this anymore," he said.

The full impact of that statement hit her. She froze. The minute she took her dress off, all her scars would be revealed. Red streaks of skin that spread out under her ribs. The roughness of them had smoothed a lot over time, but they were still visible when she was naked. Would he be disgusted by what he saw?

"Ryder? Are you all right? If you're not ready for this, that's okay. As much as I want you, I won't be mad. Tonight isn't about me. It's about us." He placed his lips against hers, soft and feathery and light. Slowly the fire in her built again, overtaking her fear.

I do want this. He can't really see my marks, it's so dark in here. "No," she finally agreed, "I don't need to wear this. She took it upon herself to wriggle out of her dress and bra until she was left with only her high-heeled sandals and lace panties. She turned around to hang up her clothes, reaching up to feel for a tack hook.

She heard him move behind her. Felt the fine hair of his chest against her back. Then she realized that was not all she felt. In the few seconds it took her to partially strip and hang her clothes he apparently had time to do the same.

But then his hands reached around her back to hold her breasts and all thought on clothing—and anything else—flew out her head.

"Do you have protection?" His voice sounded strained, no doubt like the rest of him.

She felt her face flush and was even more grateful the darkness wouldn't reveal that, either. "Um, Mindy gave me some before I left work today . . . You know how she's always kidding around. She wouldn't take it back, and I didn't want a box of condoms lying about the stalls."

Jake let out a laugh. "Yeah, that would have generated a lot of conversation. I'm sure Lenny would have had plenty to say."

Ryder muffled a giggle. "Yeah, especially considering the fact Mindy picked *ultra-sensitive super-thin French tickler magnums*."

His laughter grew into a roar. "Magnums, huh? I should thank her." His voice grew silky and seductive. "She guessed right, you know."

"Really?" she teased, her voice throaty. "I'm going to enjoy finding out." *Lord above, did I really say that?*

But she couldn't dwell on her admission because his lips were on the side of her throat again. Making her blood buzz. Making her head dizzy. Her blood pounded in her veins.

She fumbled with her dress and slipped her hand inside a pocket. Her search prompted his own exploration. The sudden sensation of his lithe fingers through her panties' thin fabric made her shiver underneath the lace.

She heard the sound of his hard breath against her neck, and then the crinkle of a wrapper as she handed him the condom, followed by the sensation of her undies falling away.

"I'm going to make love to you, Ryder Hannon. Like I've been dying to do since the moment we met." He kissed her neck as she silently nodded, his front still pressed to her back. For a brief moment his hands were off her.

She heard the sound of the tiny packet ripping open and then felt a hand wrap around her breast. "Since we're in with the horses, we should be like them."

"What do you . . .?" she started to ask. He moved her back from the wall to bend her slightly forward.

"Oh," she gasped, color rising to her cheeks. But the feel of him rubbing his hard length against her softness was too enticing to fight. He was teasing her by touching her there and then pulling back until she was twisting around to him in desperation. "Jake. Please . . ." *I shouldn't beg. What the heck is wrong with me?*

"I thought you'd never ask," he said as he pushed himself into her.

She hadn't even realized the extent of how ready she was.

"My Lord," she murmured. Then her quick breathing made it impossible to say anything more as he tormented and teased her from behind. Until he picked up a fast pace of his own.

Pleasure ripped through her body. Her legs quivered and she felt her eyes roll back in bliss. Yet he didn't pause to slow down. Nor to enjoy the sweet, building sensation. The delicious friction continued until his whole body went stiff. Then she felt his erect penis jerk and pulse inside her. His orgasm triggered her own.

They stayed interlocked for a long while until he had an obvious need to pull out. With a last kiss on her throat, he gave a short laugh. "Damn, now I know why horses do it this way."

Despite still shivering in ecstasy, she laughed. "If I ever see horses using a missionary position instead, I'll let you know."

"Do that. Though I don't think I'll need to borrow inspiration. In fact, this memory will be burnt into my brain forever." He reached over to grab her clothes. "Let's get dressed. I want to take you to my home. We're not even going to stop by your apartment to pick up your things. I have everything you need."

Yes, Jake, you do.

Chapter 9

Jake drove his Ferrari up the graveled driveway to his house. His *really* big house, if he was to be honest. Federal-style with intricate marble inlays and brickwork. The land was perfectly manicured as if surrounding a French chateau. Two fluted columns with Corinthian caps flanked the grand, mahogany wood entrance. The house was perfect. But was it a little *too* perfect? Or simply over-the-top?

He had never before thought about his ostentatious home from someone else's perspective. Or even his own perspective. His father had dictated that he buy something worthwhile, and Jake, not wanting to be bothered with trying to figure out what that meant, asked Steven to figure it out. And if Steven was baffled as to the directive, despite being a real estate broker, Dina had no hesitation at jumping in to find the correct parcel.

Jake had bought the place sight unseen, not bothering to check it out until after all the furniture was moved in. His sister had seen to all of it. Everything in tip-top order in case their father ever dropped by. As for Jake, so long as there was a place to sleep and shower, it was fine. For him, gaining wealth was about the win, not about fancy trappings.

Unfortunately, his assumption that purchasing the house would dissuade their urge to control him was a major miscalculation. Once the deed was recorded on the land records and the last of the fixtures put in, the real haranguing began. They pushed him to get "someone to share the great big, beautiful house with."

If Jake had known that, he would have stayed living in his bachelor pad in Manhattan forever. Frankly, he liked his Park Avenue penthouse better anyway. Only two bedrooms, with one used as a home office. It had more windows than it did furnishings, which suited him fine. The furniture had had simple clean lines, not the frou-frou carved wood and ornate mirrors his sister chose for the mansion. For a man who didn't much bother with interior décor, he had done a pretty good design job with his apartment, if he said so himself.

Although living in the Long Island countryside did have its advantages. Like being close to the stables so he could track his horses' progress. And impressing the heck out of women. Assuming he was, (1) on a power charge that day; and, (2) willing to play up the powerful alpha mega-millionaire role with women who would be adequately impressed by that.

He snuck a glance out of the corner of his eye at Ryder, who had fallen asleep in his car. A dreamy expression had set upon her face, basking in an afterglow he envied. His own afterglow left the minute he turned into the great circular driveway. Would Ryder be duly impressed like Betsy had been? A part of him hoped so. *Anything* to make Ryder want to be with him again.

But a part of him also hoped not. Having Ryder turn out to be just like Betsy was the exact opposite of what he needed in a woman. He had listened to his family enough. Their tastes could prevail in most ways, since most things he didn't care about. Like where, or how, he lived. Or even what lifestyle he should lead. But business deals, and now women, were hands off. All matters close to his heart would have to be far from their hands.

He stopped the car, unbuckled his seatbelt, and leaned over to kiss her awake. "Wake up, Sleeping Beauty." He watched her eyes flutter open.

She blinked hard, stretched out as best as could be done in a sports car, and fixed her gaze on the windshield. "Wow," Ryder said. "It makes sense you're Prince Charming. This place is a castle. Do you really live here?"

"No," he deadpanned.

She gave him a playful smile. "It's really owned by somebody else, all part of this big lie you're rich?"

"I'm a liar, huh? Slide your hands down my pants. Make sure they're not on fire."

"Not a bad idea." She shot him a smoky expression, as if she were on fire, too.

I need to shut up. If we keep up this banter I won't be able to wait until I get her all the way upstairs to my bedroom.

"It won't work, you know," she commented casually.

"What won't?" He scowled. *Trust me, I'm going to work fine. Just give me five seconds to get your clothes off. I sure as hell don't need any little blue pills and I'm going to prove that to you right—*

"Your ruse," she answered. "I'm sure the real owners will come back any minute. Despite your praying they won't leave their vacation condo in Belize."

"Oh my God, you've seen through my whole charade," he answered flatly. "Since we're going inside, you'll have to wonder how much I'm bribing the butler to play along with this elaborate game."

Her eyes opened wide. "You have a butler? For real?"

"Twelve of them, actually. But only Jeeves is allowed to let people in." He parked the car and walked around to hold open her door, ignoring her gaping mouth. He did his best to avert his eyes so he didn't break out into laughter.

"You're teasing me, aren't you?" she said crossly.

"Yup. Totally worth it. Your expression is priceless." The laughter he had been holding in tumbled forth, a prisoner desperate to have been set free. "I don't know why you're upset. You started it."

A slow smile spread across her face. "But when I tease, it's funny."

"Right. I'll make a note of that. My teasing is definitely not funny. So why am I laughing?" When he calmed down he grabbed her hand as they walked up the marble steps. "I don't have twelve butlers. I do have someone who lives onsite for security and maintenance purposes. He lives in a guesthouse out back. I also have two housekeepers who come several times a week. I try to keep house staff to a bare minimum. I don't love hordes of people around me. I don't trash my own house so a lot of clean-up isn't necessary. I can cook. Even throw in the occasional load of laundry. I don't mind doing a little work to keep my house all to myself. As much as possible anyway."

"You sound like a hermit. But you're not."

When he pressed the electronic keypad at the front door they entered into a foyer shaped like a rotunda.

"Your home is stunning," she marveled.

"Thanks. But I can't take credit for choosing it." He gave her a seductive smile. "I only picked the woman standing inside it. And as far as stunning is concerned, that distinction goes exclusively to you."

Warm red color flushed her pretty cheeks. "Can I check your place out?"

"Sure. Make yourself at home. Do you want anything to drink?"

"Coffee, maybe?"

"Screw that small stuff. I'll whip us up some cappuccinos. One of the perks of having a big stuffy house like this is having enough space to hold everything I want." *Like you. Wait, where did that come from?* He forced his thoughts back on-track. "I brought my cappuccino maker back from Italy last summer. There's nothing like it." He hustled over to the kitchen. "Sugar?" he called out over his shoulder.

"Sure. Thanks. I know how much effort you're going through for me. I appreciate it."

"No problem at all. Hope you like it." *And me.*

Ryder spent the time waiting for her cappuccino by wandering around the various rooms. The house was amazing. Almost out of a fairytale. She glided a fingertip lightly over a stately wood desk to see if it was real. *Can I feel things in my dreams, too?* If so, she hoped she wasn't going to wake up for a long while. Because right now, she was in a castle. With a prince. And Lord knew Jake owned enough horses for him to ride in on. Handsome Dancer was chestnut brown, not white, but both of them were certainly regal enough.

She strolled into a library room and fought against her hands' desire to pick up his many knick-knacks for inspection. The temptation was great. A million curios demanded her attention. A good many of them seemed to be awards for his contributions to different charities and non-profit business organizations. Seeing the positive way other people viewed Jake made her admire—and want—him more.

One eye-level shelf in the library had a row of picture frames displayed. Each frame was made of simple wood and all were made in the same craftsman style. Every photograph showed smiling faces. One picture was of Jake as a child standing next to an older girl. The girl had a pleasant smile and wore long light-brown braids. He and the girl appeared in many photos obviously taken throughout the years. Some pictures were with an older man whom Jake resembled, and some were with a woman whom the daughter favored. *It's clear the girl is the sister. So who was the slim, sexy woman in the most recent photo of Jake?*

This dark-haired woman sported a solitaire diamond almost as a big as the olives at the French restaurant. She stood next to a cake bearing the words, "Congrats on your engagement!" Behind her stood Jake, who held her hand. Jake's smiling eyes reached out to Ryder from the photo. All the way to the pit of her stomach. *I think I'm going to be sick.*

"There you are," Jake said, interrupting her thoughts. "I thought you got away from me. Were you nervous to try my cappuccino?"

She stared at him silently until his face scrunched up, clearly confused. He set the cups down on an antique end table. "What's wrong?"

"Nothing. I want to hear all about your engagement."

"Geez, Ryder," he answered dryly, "I know we had an extraordinarily good time back at the stables, but don't you think we should get to know each other a little bit better before you ask to marry me?"

His sarcasm eased her apprehension a little. If he could joke about the situation she must be incorrect about her assumption. "Can you answer the question seriously? Please?"

She watched his eyebrows knit together. "No, I'm not engaged. Why on earth would you ask me such a thing?" His temper was clearly kicking in, if the harsh tone of his voice was any indication. "We just had the most fantastic experience, why ruin it?"

Her lips welded together, she lifted the photo of him and the dark-haired brunette and showed it to him.

"Oh. Me and Betsy," he said softly, straightening up. "We broke up. I forgot that picture was still in here. I never come into this room. I didn't even decorate it. My sister did."

Ryder bit down on her lower lip, feeling stupid and accusatory. "Sorry to have brought it up. Since it's an engagement photo, I needed to know."

"You need to believe I'm not a liar. I would never be with a woman if I'm engaged to someone else. You need to understand that about me, or you don't understand me at all." He raked a hand through his thick hair. "I'm sorry for the photo. I'll have it removed but don't doubt me again, okay? I have enough doubts from my family. I've been searching for the one woman in life who will stand by me no matter what. That woman was not Betsy. I'm hoping it's you."

Silence permeated the air. Neither of them moved. Breathed.

"I really want to be with you, Ry. I want our relationship to grow. I'm incredibly attracted to you. But I have my own issues. Being second-guessed is one of them."

She watched him take a breath, admiring his ability to do so. Her breath had been suspended the minute she saw that photo. "You're right, I shouldn't have doubted you. I'm sorry. Like you, I have my own issues. I'm a little overprotective of myself. I try to wall myself off from things that are going to make me fail. I don't often reach out for the brass rings in life anymore. Somehow I managed to work up enough courage to reach out for you. But then I saw this picture . . ." She placed the frame back on the desk with a hard *thump*.

Jake pulled her into his arms, and she dropped her head against his chest. "I'm so sorry, Jake," she whispered.

"Shhh. It's all right. Things were a little . . . powerful between us back at the stables. We're just a little overemotional right now."

She reached her arms around him and reveled in the feeling of security and warmth.

"You know what will make us feel better?" he asked solemnly.

"No, what?"

"If we re-enact the stable scene upstairs." He let go of her and gave her a wink. Then he grabbed her hand and she followed him.

Then he stopped short. "Damn. Almost forgot about the cappuccinos. I guess we need a temporary change in our plans. First let me indulge you. Then we can indulge in each other. Deal?"

She felt a broad grin stretch across her lips. "I don't know. Pretty tempting offers either way. You say you make mighty good coffee."

He arched an eyebrow.

"Then again," she conceded, "you make mighty good love, too."

"So which will it be?"

She pretended to stroke her chin in indecision. "Which one is more worthy of my time?"

Before she could finish teasing him, he grabbed her around the waist and swung her over his shoulder. He carried her all the way up the winding staircase to the second story.

"Fairytales don't have cavemen," she pretended to chastise.

"If I'm a caveman then you are definitely my captive."

"Captive, huh? I guess I'll need a knight in shining armor to rescue me?"

"I can definitely promise you a shining night. How about I get started now?"

She giggled girlishly. "A shining night with a caveman, completely filled with sexual gratification. That's one twisted fairytale. But I like it."

When he eventually dropped her onto the soft mattress of his four-poster bed she liked it even more.

"When we kiss," he murmured, "you make me feel all crazy inside." With a slow, lazy hand that belied her own need for action he traced the contours of her breasts. She was so wrapped up in the sensation she almost missed the feeling of her garments being removed. Almost.

"Jake," she murmured, "I hate to stop this, but I need you to do something for me."

"Don't worry, I have my own box of condoms. I didn't know I could rely on Mindy." The sound of his laughter was muffled from his head on her chest.

"Glad you're so organized," she said drolly. "But I meant something else. Can you turn off the lights?"

He eyed her quizzically. "Which one of us is ugly? If it's me, I can wear both a condom and a paper bag."

"Ha ha ha. I'm serious. Please?"

"Sure thing. As soon as you explain why. What's wrong?"

"My accident . . . it left me a little . . ."

"You mean your scars?"

She felt her face heat up. Her heart pounded in her chest. Only this time from embarrassment and raw nerves.

"I know they're there. I felt them on you."

"Oh my God, you what?" She sank down lower into the bed, dragging the bedcover around her.

"Geez, Ryder, calm down. I don't care about any of that. You are beautiful. I want to see you naked."

He tugged at the blanket but her grip was iron clad. "No, okay? Please?"

"Okay. At least I'm comfortable with you seeing my body." He got up to strip off his clothes.

Good thing, the man is gorgeous. Taut muscles that had been hidden by high-end clothes were now gloriously revealed. Tight abs. Firm thighs. Built biceps. The food at Chez Louis XIV could not have been more tempting.

"If you enjoyed the preview," he teased after turning off the lights, "can we move on to the performance?"

"Technically, wouldn't this be an encore?"

"I'll show you an encore," he said as he climbed underneath the blanket.

As soon as he was on top of her she felt her skin peak and crest. Felt the heat creep up and take over. Bit her lip as his kisses worked their way down her body. Closed her eyes with an anticipation that was almost painful as he nudged his upper body down between her thighs.

"Last time was too fast. This time will be slow. I want to make love to you, Ryder Hannon. I want to revel in your heat. I want the feel of you as you embrace me. Tonight I am going to be a part of you."

From his words and the touch of his mouth, hands, and body, she floated away in a cloud of sensations.

"Hey, you're finally awake," Jake teased.

"Hmmm? What?" Ryder tried to rouse herself from a deep sleep and to kick her brain into gear. Blinking, her eyes darted around, trying to get her bearings. She was in an enormous bedroom. With Jake. Who was standing up wearing only pajama pants, smiling at her with an obvious affection so deep she felt herself blush in response.

"Morning," she finally mumbled. *Good Lord, I've slept with an owner. A well-known, well-connected, owner. Whom I work for. And who knows about all of my scars. Damn.*

"You seem a bit nervous. Are you? How are you feeling?" he asked.

"Umm. Okay." *Considering I probably have morning breath and look like a wreck in addition to everything else.*

"Not sure I believe you. But go wash up and hurry right back."

"Okay, I'm going." As soon as she pushed the blankets off of her she realized she was naked. Heat rushed to her cheeks and she ran into the bathroom. In a second, she had slammed the door behind her.

"I don't know what your problem is," he called out pleasantly. "You really are quite beautiful."

"Er, thanks," she said loudly enough to be heard through the door. "I'm nowhere close yet, but give me a few moments. I can work my way up to being presentable. I hope."

With a slump of relief to be in privacy, she made her way over to the sink. Using his toothbrush was way too intimate.

So was showing him her scars.

Chapter 10

Ryder passively watched Handsome Dancer and Golden Child being hot walked by two teenaged girls. The girls were working hard but clearly enjoying themselves, their laughter filling the air. Ryder remembered the same joy she felt when she was their age at being allowed to help with a horse's care. There had been no better feeling, until she started learning how to jockey.

She rested her forearms on the railing as she reminisced. The smell of cut grass and damp earth filled her nose. The sunlight warmed her skin. She closed her eyes to enjoy a stray breeze blowing in.

She could not believe all that had happened in the few short weeks since the night she and Jake had been together. Their relationship was progressing as fast as Handsome Dancer. Which was saying quite a lot. Handsome Dancer's desire to succeed during his practice runs was nothing less than stellar. An ordinary thoroughbred would require a resting period of a week, sometimes two, after a vigorous practice session. But after waiting only a day or two, Handsome would whimper to go out and do it again. At first she thought maybe she was misreading his signals, but his desire to take off when she mounted him could not have been clearer if he spoke English.

She thought back to Jake's teasing her that she was Dr. Doolittle. *Maybe I do speak "horse." And maybe relationships based on trust and communication do work out.*

If it did work out, she would be responsible for two miraculous performances. She had never opened herself up so completely to an animal, let alone a man. Both males had a way of getting under her skin. It felt like the soothing warmth of the sun.

Swatting away a pesky mosquito, she wondered which of the two males was more affectionate. The way their eyes looked at her soulfully hit her in the heart. Although with Jake, the sensation zinged further down . . .

"Hey, Ry," Mindy called out from across the way.

Ryder waved back with vigor. *I belong here.* She closed her eyes again, reveling in the bliss of the perfect afternoon. So far, everything was going well. Tomorrow, Handsome Dancer would be entered in a race. Emanuel Velasquez would be the jockey. Would all her good luck continue?

The next afternoon was hotter than Hades around the racetrack. Jake, however, failed to notice either the weather or its effect. He had bigger things on his mind. Like the upcoming race, Handsome Dancer's first.

The bugler played "The Call to the Post," effectively announcing the start of the race. Spectators moved to take their seats in the public viewing stands. The massive arena was surprisingly packed for an end-of-season, average Saturday. It was a pleasure to see so many spectators after the Belmont Stakes three weeks before. Usually after the final stop of the Triple Crown, the crowds died down a bit. It was possible the long-awaited triumph of American Pharoah had given horseracing in general, and the New York Racing Association in particular, a popularity boost.

He could only hope Handsome Dancer would eventually earn the same whirlwind worldwide love. Though several of Jake's stallions had done quite well in notable races with large pots, things with a particular horse had to happen in their own natural order. If Handsome did well today, he could try him out some more in Saratoga. The Upstate New

York track's season would start shortly. A few wins there would solidify Handsome Dancer's spot back at Belmont.

His thoughts drifted to upcoming summer nights with his lovely lady. They would stroll along Saratoga's main street after the afternoon races were done, hand-in-hand. What he needed was patience. Too bad it was in short supply. He could barely wait for the race to start, let alone for Ryder to fall headlong into his arms. He glanced down at his watch. *The race should be starting any second now.*

A bead of sweat slowly trickled down his neck as he stood against the rail of the owner's VIP viewing section. A droplet fell onto his chest, but he swatted the sensation away as if it were a pesky summer fly. His gaze, and complete focus, were now on the scene unfolding in front of him. He squinted through the intense sunlight, a hand over his eyes in a futile attempt to block out the glare.

The massive television screen out on the field showed the starting gate roughly six furloughs away, impossible to see clearly with the naked eye.

The digital screen showed the gates open and then a blur of horses. The stallions had taken off like mini tornados.

Jake's fingers went tightly into fists. The announcer's voice filled the massive arena. *"And they're off, ladies and gentlemen . . ."*

A moment later, he nearly bit the inside of his mouth from nerves as he realized Handsome Dancer, still standing in the eighth gate, was the last to leave. The horse's hesitation lasted two heart-stopping seconds. Then he bolted, with Emanuel in the saddle, flying at such speed they were no more than a streak of brown as they raced past each mile-marker post on the outside of the track.

Jake's heart hit against his ribcage hard enough to put a jackhammer to shame. And it only got worse as Handsome Dancer evened up with the other contenders, and then left them way behind. The closest horse to him had its nose behind Handsome Dancer's tail.

Handsome Dancer moved to the inside, as close to the rail as he could get. Emanuel obviously had used great skill in getting him there, weaving in and out of the wall of traffic to place Handsome solidly in the lead.

But then Handsome Dancer faltered. Jake watched in horror as his horse stumbled then was smacked from behind against his outside flank. Both horses almost fell over before recovering. Emanuel, however, had less luck. The capable jockey bounced off Handsome Dancer's back. And onto the dirt track.

Jake's heart almost stopped. His breathing halted. The crowd gasped. He watched helplessly as Emanuel lay still, no doubt praying he wouldn't be trampled to death. The other jockeys did what they could to avoid tragedy, but stopping a sea of stampeding horses, all spooked from the accident, was no easy feat. Even for the best.

After what seemed an eternity, Emanuel managed to roll himself over to the guardrail and to the safety of the soft turf inside the Winchester track. Applause broke out from the spectators. Belmont's ambulance, the one that drove along the track of every race, stopped. Paramedics jumped out and within seconds Emanuel was whisked away.

The announcer's voice came on. "The ambulance workers gave us the thumbs-up. Emanuel Velazquez is going to be all right folks . . ." The crowd cheered loudly.

Jake felt air go into his lungs. He took off for the stairway leading down to the track.

Despite the injury, the race had continued on. Rider-less Handsome Dancer, however, had slowed his pace. By the time he come to a complete stop, the other thoroughbreds were safely past him and headed down the home stretch.

Jake held his breath as the announcer's voice came on over the loudspeaker again. One of Barney Smythe's horses,

Big Pay Day, had won the race. Handsome Dancer and the horse that had bumped him had been disqualified.

Jake fought the hordes to get himself out on the track to grab Handsome Dancer's reins. Until he noticed Ryder had beaten him there. She held Handsome's reins loosely as she checked him over.

If the horse had any injury or distress from the ordeal, he didn't show it. Ryder's face, however, did. "I think Handsome is okay. I'm so sorry for what happened to Emanuel though. I hope he really is going to be all right. The paramedics say he's conscious and only broke his leg. Unfortunately, they think it's in two places." She grimaced. "They're going to check him over for a concussion, too."

A zillion photoflashes went off around him. "Great. This will be all over ESPN," he muttered. "Give us some quiet, folks. Can't you see a man was hurt?"

The unfazed paparazzi, however, continued taking their shots.

When the crowd was finally gone, and Handsome Dancer was walked off the track by a hostile Lenny, Ryder put an arm around Jake. "I know you're upset for Emanuel, but he's going to be okay. Considering how fast Handsome Dancer was going, Emanuel's lucky he didn't get killed."

"You're right," he conceded. "I'll check on him as soon as the medics let me." Jake let out a hard breath and gestured over to his horse. "How is he?"

"I'm sure he's spooked, but he'll be okay, too."

There was something about her calm, quiet nature he always found so soothing. On a *craptastic* day like today, her soothing nature was even more appreciated than usual. He took Ryder's free hand and walked with her away from the track and back to the stables.

Chapter 11

It had been several days since Emanuel's fall. Handsome Dancer had been too skittish to be ridden since then. Emanuel's attitude fared not much better. Jake handled the last phone call from the jockey with a combination of sympathy and anger. The sympathy had been expected, but not the anger. Emanuel was somehow convinced Ryder's poor training skills had caused the horse to stumble. No amount of persuasion could change the jockey's mind. Jake held his head in his hand, bracing against a migraine as he recalled their multiple conversations.

"She doesn't know what she is doing," the jockey had accused.

"Any horse can stumble at any time," Jake had countered. "You know that. It's one of the risks of being a jockey. This sport is dangerous."

"It *is* dangerous. That's why nobody hires a woman to do it."

"Sexist accusations aren't going to help either of us, Emanuel. You know there are other women trainers out there. I've even seen another one in the stables, a Mindy somebody-or-other."

"There's no need for me to know their names because they cannot do the job right."

Those telephone calls had been almost as painful as the subsequent one with his father. "I told you that horse is a loser," his father challenged.

"You say that about everything I value."

"I'm always right, aren't I?" His father didn't pause long enough for Jake to respond. "I don't approve of you dating this trainer, either. People are starting to talk about it. Important people. Ones who go to our country club."

"Good for them," Jake tossed out, trying to sound much more cavalier than he felt.

"Jake," his father warned in an ominous tone. "One of the things I'm right about is Ryder Hannon. Obviously her training skills aren't worth a good God—"

"Don't say it," Jake hissed. "I'm getting tired of listening to people who grasp onto any excuse they can dredge up as to why it's Ryder's fault. Maybe the fault lies with the track's field condition. Or the jockey—"

"I doubt it was the track. If anybody saw anything irregular in the field conditions an announcement would have been made. As for the jockey, you're the one who picked him and I wouldn't have done that, either. But you're right about one thing. It could have been his fault. Fire him and then fire the girl."

Jake did his best to stop the brewing explosion inside him. "Ryder Hannon is a grown woman, not a girl."

"She looks like a lost waif."

"Are you making fun of her appearance? She was a jockey. She still maintains a jockey's figure."

"She doesn't look womanly. Although clearly you're able to think of her as a woman. No doubt that's why you're sleeping with her," his father grumbled.

Jake's voice lowered an octave. "Back off from my sex life, Dad. It's none of your bus—"

"Oh, but it is my business. Because a large part of my money is funding your operations."

"I have supported myself for years. Want a check to reimburse you for the rest of it? I'll send one right off," he spat through tight lips.

"Watch it, son. Here's another piece of business advice you need. You get rid of the girl, not the father. Stop screwing the hired help and put your focus back where it belongs."

Jake slammed the house phone down so hard a sconce on the mahogany-paneled wall rattled.

Ten minutes later, he lifted his head out of his hands and got up to get some aspirin. The throbbing in his head wouldn't go away. He could only hope the rest of his problems would. It didn't seem likely though. He could maybe live without the family support. But he couldn't without a jockey.

Ryder stared at Jake in the mansion's great white kitchen, blinking hard in disbelief. "A present? For me? You know my birthday isn't until November. What's the occasion?"

"Open it and find out. I'm getting antsy to give it to you." He gestured to the wrapped gift on the counter.

"Don't have to ask me twice." Ryder tore it open to find a silk jacket inside with a matching helmet cover. Red and yellow harlequin diamonds shone brightly against a white background. Realization hit her with a force so strong she felt it in her stomach. *Oh!*

"Yup. Jockey silk in the colors of my stables. It's the most perfect gift I could ever get you. I would be honored if you'd wear this jacket."

Her mouth hung open, not moving.

"I have faith in you, Ry. Now you need to have faith in you, too. Pick up the gauntlet I'm throwing down."

"You really want me to do this? Now?"

"You heard me. We have a big race coming up. The one Handsome Dancer was practicing for, the last race of Belmont's season. I want you to be the jockey."

She moved her jaw up and down but it took a few moments for words to come out. "Think about this, Jake. Handsome Dancer is still very skittish after what happened during this last race."

"He'll be willing to race. I know it. And we both know he's not going to let anyone else ride him besides you. Is he?"

Ryder thought about the men she had encouraged to take over for Emanuel. Rafael Ladeaux was thrown off halfway around the track in a practice run. The man was lucky he was only superficially injured. John Litton could not even persuade Handsome to move. Mike Barton made the most progress, he got Handsome Dancer to sulk around the entire track.

"I know Handsome will let you ride him," Jake persuaded. "You know it, too."

Ryder shook her head. But even as she did, she knew Jake was right. She had ridden Handsome Dancer successfully since Emanuel's fall and had the same astonishing results as her first practice run.

But being a jockey again? No way. Not. Gonna. Happen. "I'll find somebody," she promised. *There's got to be somebody.*

"No, you won't. So let's go with the person I found. You."

She stepped back from him and crossed her arms over her chest. "Impossible. I'm a trainer, not a jockey."

He arched an eyebrow at her. "You still have your jockey license, don't you? C'mon, Ryder. I know deep down you want to do this."

She sucked her lips into her mouth and bit down. "Lose? No, I don't want to do that at all."

"Are you trying to convince you or me that you're going to fail?"

"What would people say?" she cried out, circumventing the question. "People will think you've lost your mind. First, for betting on a loser horse, and then for betting on a loser jockey." Her voice sounded strangled. "Your father called me today. Told me he'd pay me to not train Handsome Dancer anymore. I'd get the equivalent of three months' worth of winnings, just by giving up."

"My father did *what*?"

"I wouldn't have told you if you didn't bring this up. I don't want to cause any more trouble."

"You? It's my crazy, controlling father who is causing trouble." His lips twisted into a flat smirk. "I'm going to enjoy the phone call I make to him tonight. It's time he understands he'd better let me handle my own business."

"I agree, he's definitely controlling, but in his mind, maybe he's also trying to help you. Stop your financial bleeding before the patient dies." Her voice got very quiet. "I'm trying to protect you, too, Jake. I'm not going to risk your investment by riding."

"Why is everyone trying to decide what's best for me? I need to make my own choices. I choose to let Handsome Dancer race, whether or not my father likes it. And I choose you to be Handsome's jockey, if you'll willing to take the chance. I'm not pressuring you, Ryder, but I'm sure as hell not going to accept your refusal because somehow you think you're doing me a favor."

Ryder clutched her arms around herself tighter. She was now feeling cold. "What would people think?"

"I'll tell them that as far as I'm concerned, the longer the odds the more I like it. Big money gambles big." He laughed, although there was little mirth in his voice. "Who cares what they think? Or what I tell them? People, like my father, will believe what they want to anyway. The only person's mind I want to change is yours. You need to believe you can do this. Be the person you always wanted to be. Not because I want you to race but because you want to."

"I . . . I don't know."

"Think about it," he said. He stepped forward and pulled her close to him until their bodies were joined from chest to knees. Leaning over, he kissed the top of her forehead. "This is a chance both of us need to take. I need to show my father I'm going to follow my own path. You are going to show yourself, and all the naysayers out there, that you are one hell of a jockey. Win or lose, you'll have proven you're made of tough stuff."

"I don't want to prove myself to anyone."

"How about to yourself?"

"I like you, Jake," she said softly. "But don't make me sorry I opened up to you. I may have wanted to be a jockey once upon a time. But I've moved on. Changed my goals. Changed me. I have a safe, viable business now. I'm respected more as a trainer than I ever was as a jockey. It may not be easy being a woman trainer, but as a jockey I was a laughing stock. Even before I fell off a horse and became an even bigger joke."

"Emanuel fell of a horse. Nobody thinks he's a laughing stock."

"Of course not. He's a man."

"Maybe nobody was laughing at you, either. You perceived them to be laughing because you think they scorn all women riders."

Ryder swallowed hard and crossed her arms over her chest. "It's not my *perception*. It's a fact. Barney Smythe may have done you favors by selling Handsome Dancer for a song, but he never did any favors for me. He went right up to me after my fall and told me I was making the entire sport of horseracing look bad. That I should quit if I cared about the sport at all."

Jake's eyes went wide. "He actually said that to you? What an ass. Did you have some kind of connection with him that he thought he could approach you in the first place?"

"His cousin was the one I was riding for. I guess Barney thought it was a matter of family pride."

"Now I'm even happier I have his horse."

"Sure, you'll make him feel stupid if Handsome Dancer wins. But if I ride him, not only can I fail, he'll make a laughing stock out of you, too. You're not a family member Barney will want to protect. You'll be the guy who was dumb enough to hire a female jockey. One with a poor track record."

He smiled slowly. "So what? My father already thinks something similar. I'm either too stubborn or stupid to follow his advice." He laughed. "Or both."

Ryder felt her heart grow heavy. "It's even worse that your father thinks less of you than he does me."

"I respect my father, but he's narcissistic. He thinks the only way to success is to follow directly in his footprints. It kills him when I trail blaze. He thinks I set myself up for failure. But I love a good challenge. Who wants to live life in someone else's shadow?"

Ryder stayed quiet. *How ironic. I'd love to live in my father's shadow. Follow along in his footprints. Live up to the name he gave me.* Her gaze dropped to the floor. *He tried so hard to back me. Our dream was the same. It's so sad to have to let that dream go . . .*

"Are you all right, Ry? You're shivering and the color's gone from your face." He gestured to the cappuccino cups he'd laid out on the countertop. "Maybe you should drink yours. It'll warm you up." When she didn't move, he picked up the mug that was closest to him. "I'll demo it for you. Show you it's not vile." He took a long sip. "Fantastic, if I do say so myself. Remember I only buy my coffee machines from Italy. Life is too short for sub-standard."

The rich and fragrant aroma of coffee filled the air. It was tantalizing but she declined. "I'm too tensed up for caffeine. Jake, I don't want to be the cause of a rift between you and your father. Any more than I already am."

He held the cup in his hands, obviously mulling over her statement. "There's already a rift between us. I don't like being told what I can and cannot do. I also don't like him going behind my back. He never should have called you.

He's always been dogmatic, but meddling into my affairs, and yours, was crossing the line."

"It's not only your father who doubts my ability." She watched Jake put the cup to his lips again, envious his stomach wasn't too sour to drink it.

"I've been stuck my whole life listening to my father," he said. "But what's your excuse? I'm surprised you'd listen to him or a guy like Barney Smythe. Barney came right out and told you that women can't be jockeys, and you listened to him. Still do."

"That's not fair. It's just that I . . ."

Jake placed the cup back on the countertop. "It's just what, Ryder? That he's right? Right because you had an accident, so you have to toss away your whole career? Men have accidents all the time. No one tells them they can't ride. It's the jockey who's supposed to decide when to retire."

"Okay, I decided, and I'm telling you my career is through." Her eyes were starting to water and sting. "I don't want to discuss this anymore."

"Talking this out is the only way to resolve it."

"It's resolved."

"Really? Glad you've agreed to be my jockey. Excellent!"

She narrowed her eyes, swiping away the wetness in a corner. "You know what I meant."

"Yes, I do. You meant our discussion is over. But I'm not ready to let the topic drop. What are you so afraid of?"

"Can't you let it go?"

"Sure. After you answer me."

"I'm afraid of failing! Of having my best efforts fall short. To want something so badly, only to be horribly disappointed." Her voice broke. "Okay? Are you happy now?" The tears ran down her face. Her nose ran. She gave a loud sniff and angrily wiped her face with the back of her hand. "Do you know what it is to be the daughter of a world famous jockey? Not the son, but the daughter?"

He stood silently as he watched her. After a moment, he placed his hand on hers but she snatched it back.

"You never saw all the pity people gave him." Her voice sounded far away, almost as if she were talking to herself. "People couldn't believe the irony that he had only one child, and it had to be a girl. They would shake their head sadly with a look that said *what a waste*." She gulped down the saliva pooling in her throat. "It would have been hard enough if I were a boy, always trying to prove I was worthy to follow a legend. Imagine what I had to endure being a *girl* trying to follow in his footsteps."

She fiddled with the cappuccino cup in front of her but didn't pick it up. "My father really put himself out on a limb by backing me. Risking his own reputation to help mine. And after he did all that, even fighting with people who had been some of the same owners he'd jockeyed for, what did I do? I went ahead and messed it all up, that's what."

Jake took back her hand and held it in his. His skin felt soft, smooth, and very warm. It was strangely comfortable, as if a second skin. "Everybody makes mistakes, Ry."

"*Ry* is what my dad called me. Lenny won't use it, he thinks it sounds corny." She let out a tight laugh. "Mindy, however, loves it. Especially because it gets under Lenny's skin."

"She likes to torment him, doesn't she?" His lips twisted in amusement.

She smiled, grateful for the tiny reprieve from a heavy topic. "Yeah. Lenny's so dour, he's a perfect set-up for Mindy's devilish streak. The more aggravated with her he gets, the more she's determined to roast his goose. But she's a good person. She teases, but it's never malicious. Her humor is just a little bit off."

"How so?"

"Like with my nickname. She bought me a loaf of rye bread one birthday. Put it in a box as if it were a real gift, wrapped it up and everything. She said the expression on my face when I opened it was priceless." Remembering the day, Ryder let out a slow smile. "I'm sure it was. But later on that night she took me out to a lovely restaurant for dinner and gave me an actual gift. It was a cute top I had been eyeing in a little boutique. I had forgotten I told her I liked it when we went window-shopping a few weeks before."

"At least Mindy's gifts are useful. Rye bread. A condom . . ."

Ryder laughed. "Yeah, that's Mindy for you."

"You seem to like her a lot."

"She's great. Mindy was there for me when my dad died. I took the news badly and retreated into myself for a while. She constantly did her best to pull me out of my funk. Dragged me out of the stables to make sure I stayed social. Even if it was simply getting a bite to eat with her." Ryder sniffed hard. "Her patience in dealing with me was fantastic. Dealing with a depressed person isn't easy. I mean, my mother was there for me, but she was in the same boat. Lenny, too. He's been a part of my family since before I was born. I know he loves me. He loved my dad, too. Lenny is the strong, silent type though. Not the kind of person who you talk about your feelings with. He's stoic, believing people should power through adversity. I admire him for that. And Mindy, too. She didn't have to put up with me at all."

She felt heat rise up to her cheeks. *Is he going to think I'm some sort of depressed socially-deficient freak now?*

Hesitantly, she lifted her gaze to judge his reaction. Her breathing became lighter when she didn't find him looking put-off. On the contrary, his expression was open, his eyes round with concern. "I understand why you think so much of her. Tell me, does she think you should go back to jockeying?"

Ryder paused, her tongue leaden. "Yes," she said, her voice barely audible. "Because she views my dad's death differently than I do."

Jake's brow furrowed. "I don't follow what you're saying."

"My father died from an unexpected heart attack. Mindy says I should believe what the doctors said about him having a congenital heart defect. But I don't think they're right. The real cause was all the stress he had from racing."

"You believe stress from being a jockey killed your father?"

She nodded. "Not only from his being on the track." She raked a hand through her hair. "From watching my fall. My failed race was the last one my father saw—he died a month later."

"I don't believe your fall is what inadvertently killed your father, Ry. I'm sure watching you race made him proud."

How could he have been proud? Even though he loved her unconditionally. There must have been a part of him that had wondered why she couldn't live up to both of their names. The belief she let down the man she admired most was a pain sharper than any of the severe cuts that had ripped her up. The one scar that time would not heal.

"Maybe you should listen to both of us," Jake added. "Like Mindy, I care about you. I wouldn't steer you wrong, either." He pulled her against him and kissed her, light but firm on the mouth. "Have faith in me, Ry. Better still, have faith in yourself."

A flood of emotions washed over her. A tidal wave of force.

Of all the ones that came crashing down, which emotions should she react to first? The emotional intimacy? The physical intimacy?

"It's funny," she murmured against his mouth. "Hearing my nickname come from your lips. It makes me feel like . . ."

"I really care for you? I do." He slipped his hands around her and picked her up. One arm supporting her upper body, one arm under her knees.

She yelped. "Oh! Where are we going?"

"A place where I can best show you how much I care."

"Hmmm, your bedroom. I've already been there."

"Nope. Back to your place so you can pack."

She struggled to get down from his arms. "Pack? Where are we going? No matter who rides Handsome Dancer, we've still got his race lined up."

"We're taking a fast trip to Saratoga. We'll be back in time. Can Lenny run everything by himself while you're gone?"

She nodded, speechless.

"Good. Then I'm going to inspire you to get back in the saddle. No matter what it takes."

Chapter 12

Jake marveled at how an almost five-hour road trip to Saratoga seemed to take only half an hour. The time flew by, and not only because his Ferrari was flagrantly disregarding the Taconic Parkway's posted speed limits. It was the conversation with Ryder that had made the time pass so pleasurably. They laughed while he drove and snacked at diners that had clearly seen better days. Areas to pull off the road were limited so the selections had not been good. One rest stop offered nothing but ice cream. He'd been only too happy to share the cone of mint chocolate chip that she had stared at with envy. Not that he hadn't teased her about it.

"Go buy your own," he'd barked, pretending to shield the cone from her as if he were a running back with a football.

"I don't want my own. I want some of yours."

He'd arched an eyebrow at her. "You want to lick something that's mine? Sorry, you'll have to wait until tonight."

She put her hands on her hips. "Very funny. I'm trying to keep my jockey's figure intact. If I eat a whole ice cream cone the track's 126 pound weight limit will be blown for sure."

Suddenly Jake was not laughing anymore. "You mean you are going to jockey?"

She frowned. "I don't know. Let's not talk about it anymore. Please?"

He tilted the ice cream to her and let her eat it until she handed it back. Absently he licked around the cone to catch an errant drip. The movement prevented him from breaking out into a full-blown grin. At least she was considering it.

An hour had passed. With any luck, she hadn't yet changed her mind. It would be his job for the next twenty-four hours to make sure he drove her all the way to "Yes Town." Not just for jockeying, either, but for her desire to be with him. The more time he spent with the woman, the more he wanted her. Even a would-be boring car ride seemed like a thrilling amusement park ride when he was with her. He couldn't remember the last time he'd enjoyed casual conversation so much.

It was almost a shame they had reached their first destination. "Ah, the racetrack. Finally. You can see the edge of Saratoga's course here on the left. I'm sure you're familiar with it," he commented cheerfully.

"Sure, but why is your right turn signal on?" she asked, confusion apparent in her voice.

"Because we're not going to the racetrack. Since the season up here doesn't start for another three weeks, why bother? Our first stop is actually right here," he said, pulling around a building with a horse statue out front. Big glass windows showed jockey silks from all the Triple Crown winners of the past.

"The National Museum of Racing and Hall of Fame? What a fabulous choice," she remarked with enthusiasm.

"Glad you like my idea. There's an exhibit I want you to see." He drove his Ferrari around the back of the building and parked. "Ever been here before?" he asked as they entered.

"Once. When I was younger. They had a plaque installed in their Hall of Fame with my father's name on it." Her voice trailed off. "I haven't been back since. Too many reminders of him, you know?"

He reached for her hand and she took it, giving him a shaky grin. "I love this idea. Thank you. I'm really touched you took me here in honor of my dad."

"To be honest, that's only part of the reason I took you here. It's another exhibit I want us to focus on."

He led her first to the Hall of Fame where they paused to read her father's plaque. Then viewed his jockey silks high up in a display case. Jake withdrew his smart phone and took a picture of her standing underneath her father's attire. She posed with a toothy, if somewhat sad, grin.

Then they meandered past the mannequins demonstrating a jockey's life. Some were of jockeys being weighed. Others demonstrated life in a jockey's room.

They wandered around all the trophy cups. And then past all the paintings showing the most famous horses that ever lived.

When they got to the next room Jake chirped cheerfully, "Here it is."

He watched Ryder walk up and her eyes widen at the display. *Women Jockeys in History*. "One day," he promised, "this display will feature you."

He felt her fingers tighten around his. Jake squeezed right back.

"Thank you so much for taking me to the museum," Ryder said later when they were back in his Ferrari.

"We'll have a great time in downtown Saratoga Springs, too," he promised.

Downtown Saratoga was a Victorian-era main street interspersed with modern day touches. Gingerbread architecture adorned historic brick buildings. The town was truly a step out of time.

Throngs of people walked the sidewalks. Women wearing pearls and diamonds, clearly wealthy horse owners, were mixed in with tie-dye wearing Gerry Garcia wannabes. Somehow, everybody seemed to belong.

On the streets, new Ferraris, like Jake's, were parked next to Volvos manufactured twenty years ago. Decked out

Harley Davidsons, bicycles, and even adult tricycles were scattered throughout. Once in a while an antique car could be spotted.

Dozens of street musicians played, some of their tunes clashing from playing in close proximity. Fresh flowers were everywhere, planted in urns on the street or in baskets hanging from restaurant pergolas. Decorative racetrack furlong posts and jockey statues stood in front of stores like silent sentries. Life-sized sculptures of thoroughbred horses were colorfully painted in unique, often funny designs. People stopped to marvel at one horse sculpture in particular. Titled "I'm Too Little To Ride," the horse was painted with brightly colored rainbows and ice cream cones.

"This place is bustling," she marveled.

"Yeah, and it's not even high season yet. Wait until August when things really heat up. I'm sure the good restaurants are already booked up for dinner the night of the Travers."

They spent time wandering around the boutiques, bookstores and independent coffee houses. She periodically stopped to admire jewelry and clothing.

"Planning on buying anything today?" Jake eventually asked. "Some of these items would be very pretty on you."

When he said words like that she felt her heart warm and her cheeks flush. "Thanks. No purchases yet though. I love window shopping but nothing's truly caught my eye."

"Let me know when it does so I can weigh in. If you'll let me."

Wow. A man who doesn't mind when his girlfriend shops.

The thought made her stiffen. *Am I his girlfriend?* Not sure she wanted the answer, she smiled wanly and moved on. Until they came across a hat boutique, Hat Sational.

"Oh my Lord," she practically squealed, grabbing Jake by the hand and dragging him in. "Derby hats. They're beautiful."

The tiny store had hundreds of handmade hats. Some graced mannequins, others hung from hat-racks. Each was spectacularly adorned. They donned colorful ribbons, bows, butterflies, feathers, gauze, or lace. Some were small, some had brims that were wide enough to cover three people.

"See something you like?" asked a dignified lady wearing a white derby hat trimmed with pink ribbon and turquoise feathers. Tacked onto her brim was a life-sized ladybug.

"I like everything in here," Ryder gushed.

Jake laughed. "Same goes for me. Although my date's level of enthusiasm is hard to duplicate."

The saleswoman smiled. "I'm glad you appreciate quality. What kind of hat are you looking for?"

"The one you're wearing is beautiful. The detail is outstanding. How much is it?"

"Two thousand dollars. Without the additional New York State sales tax, of course. Would you like to see which colors we have available?"

Ryder felt her stomach clench and frowned. "As much as I love the hat, I've got to admit that's way out of my price range."

The saleswoman smiled. "We also have less expensive price points for our one-of-a-kind inventory. Look around and let me know if you'd like me to price anything else for you."

The saleslady left them to browse.

"You're not going to let me buy it for you, right?" Jake asked quietly.

"No, I'm not. But thank you for offering. It's very sweet of you. However, I respect your wallet as much as I do mine. Two thousand dollars is a month's rent in Queens. I'm living in the stable hands' quarters because my landlord decided to sell the building I was in. I hated moving out, my apartment had a really nice set up. I still haven't found another nice place that isn't going to drain my bank account dry. I'm tinkering with whether to ante up for a down payment on a house but haven't decided yet."

"What kind of house?"

She laughed. "Don't worry. Not one nearly as big as yours. Come on, we might as well get going. We passed a coffee house two blocks down that's calling my name."

"Sure," he answered. "You go ahead. I've got to make a quick call, and I'll meet you there in a few minutes."

"Okay," she quipped happily as she exited the shop.

The minute Ryder left the shop, Jake called over the saleswoman. "How fast can you make a hat?"

"We don't actually make these hats. Some are made by well-known designers. Others we design ourselves on hat frames we buy. We can custom decorate those however you need."

"Okay. How fast can it be done? Tomorrow?"

The sales woman arched an eyebrow. "We can work all night, but that kind of client attention does not come cheap. Are you sure you wouldn't rather see what we have in inventory?"

"Do you have one in white, yellow, and red? Preferably with a diamond pattern somewhere in there?"

"No. I do have one in a solid navy and another decorated in cream and brown."

"I need it done my way. How about three thousand dollars if you can do it by tomorrow at 9:00 a.m.?"

The saleslady stuck out her hand. "Deal. Do you have any pictures so I'm sure of the exact hues and shape of the diamond pattern?"

"Yes." He fumbled around with his wallet for a business card, then grabbed one and handed it to her. "The symbol for Carter Stables. Come as close to this as you can."

Glancing down at the card her eyes went wide. "Yes, Mr. Carter, of course."

"Fantastic. Thanks." He handed her his credit card. "Ring it through and I'll be on my way. Have the hat dropped off at the Saratoga Arms, where we're staying."

Moments later, he was off to Uncommon Grounds to meet Ryder.

"Don't enjoy your coffee too much," Jake warned.

"We paid for it but can't enjoy it?" Ryder asked playfully. "Seems like a waste of money to me, even for a guy who drives a Ferrari."

"It's because I don't want to waste money that we have to go. I booked a spa treatment for you at the Roosevelt Bath & Spa. Ever been there?"

"No, I haven't. But I've heard of it." She grinned. "If you're trying to woo me, it's working."

Jake smiled. "Is that all it's going to take for my wooing to work? Because if it is, I'll buy the spa right now."

"It's a historic spa, isn't it? Right in Saratoga Spa State Park. I'm sure it's not for sale. Not even for you, Mr. Megabucks."

"Are you teasing me?"

"No way. I never tease. Just don't make an offer to buy the place in front of me. It'll be embarrassing."

"Finally. A weapon to lord over you. Excellent." He laughed. "Let's go."

Ryder was by herself, having been left by Jake as soon as he checked her into the brick-laid Roosevelt Bath House. This historic building, like all the others in the park, was retrofitted with some modern fixtures. An eclectic blend of old and new that managed to beautifully work together.

When Ryder's name was called by the spa staff she was shown into a small private room with a sunken bathtub, upholstered chair, and a massage table. The tile, tub, and chair looked original for the time. In fact, the whole room felt like a time warp. "Is this room original?" she asked.

"The whole room, including the bathtub, is original. Only the paint color on the wall has been changed since the 1930's."

"Wow." Ryder was duly impressed until she noticed the dark brown water in the tub. Her eyes went wide. "Um, is the water supposed to look like that?"

"Yes, don't worry. The water's brown from all the minerals," the attendant explained. "You'll soak for forty minutes so they seep into your body. The spring water has been warmed up for you but try not to make it any hotter, it'll dilute the amount of minerals and make the bath less effective."

Ryder gave the water a doubtful look and clutched the spa's oversized robe around her tighter.

"Trust me, you'll love it," the attendant assured. "You're very petite so you might bounce around from all the bubbles. Try to anchor yourself with this," she said, handing over a blue plastic stool. "Place this against the back of the tub and push back on it with your feet. It'll help keep you from floating around."

"I'll float from all the bubbles? Really?"

The woman nodded. "The water is naturally carbonated. When you're in there you can pretend you're floating in a giant glass of champagne. Have fun. I'll knock when the time is over and give you a warm fresh towel. When you're all dried off we'll start your massage." The attendant turned to leave.

"Wait, Miss—" Ryder put an arm out to touch the attendant's shoulder.

"Yes?"

"Do these mineral baths really work?"

The woman stopped and smiled. "For most people they do. Some folks find it helps them quite a lot. Some only a little. Even the ones who don't feel physically improved enjoy the experience anyway."

"What does the water do?"

"Soothes frayed nerves. Relaxes muscles and heals damage. Reduces bone aches and stomach ailments. There are also minerals in there that treat all kinds of skin conditions. They soften up rough or damaged skin so much you'd think it belongs on a baby."

This time Ryder's eyes grew even wider. "Really?"

"For some people," she confirmed. "Maybe for you, too. Let me know. In the meantime, there's a call button on the wall to push if you need me." The woman shut the door behind her.

Ryder stood alone for a minute, hesitating before she took off her robe. *Can I be this lucky?* Ryder put the stool down next to the tub and gingerly stepped in. *Here goes nothing.*

The submersion in the tub was deeper than she thought, the water level rose up to her neck. After a moment of trying to settle in, the bubbles kicked up. Not enough to be too visible but enough to lift her body. Her legs, arms, and breasts rose up to the water's surface.

Placing the stool as instructed allowed her to stay straight and secure. With her head against the back of the tub, she closed her eyes. Stress drifted away. Pleasant thoughts drifted in.

The bubbles felt so good against her skin. They floated and popped at a slow steady pace. Some popped against her scars. She peered down into the water but could not see the blemishes, or anything else, through the dark-brown liquid.

Amazing. People have been sitting here in this exact same tub for almost a hundred years. Some folks must have wanted mental relaxation. Some no doubt wanted physical relief. And some prayed for the deepest healing. Healing they longed for. Like her.

Lying in the dark waters of the barely lit room, she felt the bubbles lift not only her body but her spirits. In the dark, her body was as flawless as everybody else's. Only those close to her would ever know the marks were even there. Those people had always accepted her battle scars because they accepted her.

Was Jake one of those people? He hadn't seen her scars dead on, but he knew they were there. Surely he, too, accepted her, flaws and all.

Could she accept her flaws as well? Conquer her fear of not living up to people's high expectations? Or her own high expectations?

Chapter 13

Jake sipped a cappuccino on the patio of the Gideon Putnam Hotel, waiting for Ryder to finish her bath and massage. The hotel was historic and elegant, a stone's throw from the Roosevelt Bath House. Once she was done having her spa treatments, he'd pick her up so they could enjoy a night on the town.

Ryder was right, his mission was to win her over. Not just her body, but her mind. Like a thoroughbred racehorse, Ryder was skittish. There were walls around her for some reason. They would be tough to break through.

The whole purpose of this trip was for him to chisel away at her defenses. The spa treatment would hopefully get her relaxed enough to be receptive to what he had to say. Getting her to trust him would be hard. He'd take the help where he could get it. If it came in the form of bath water, so be it.

It was clear she wanted to be a jockey again. Equally clear, she was terrified. The thought that people judged her dream harshly paralyzed her.

For some reason she seemed to think people judged her appearance harshly, too. Sure she was petite, but she was athletically built with a beautiful face to match. Her torso was somewhat scarred up, but who cared?

He'd never been one to judge a woman's appearance unkindly. Ironically, she was, even if directed only toward herself. Her struggle to keep her body hidden, even from his eyes, made him wonder what was in her head.

Jake checked the time on his Rolex, drained the bottom of the white mug, placed a twenty-dollar bill on the table, and got up to leave. Ryder's spa time should finally be up. With any luck she'd already be dressed. He'd made dinner reservations at one of the best restaurants in town, The Patio at 15 Church. Reservations there were not easy to come by. If they were late for their eight o'clock table it would be gone. Snatched up by the next horse owner ready to descend on it like a bird of prey.

The day had been more fantasy than reality to Ryder. The last stop had been drinks and dinner at one of the best hot spots in town. The Patio at 15 Church had been more than merely a place for great cocktails, it had been a romantic wonderland. Overhead fans from the open-air pergola created a light breeze through the otherwise stifling hot night air. Instrumental music played softly through hidden loudspeakers. Rock wall fountains glowed in ever changing lights. She had sipped her Burke's Lemonade slowly, savoring every minute of the bubbly vodka drink, while watching the fountain's lights bathe the wall in pinks, purples, golds, and blues.

Jake had held her hand while they enjoyed the drinks and each other. Their conversation had flowed as easily as the water in the multi-colored rock wall.

It had almost been a shame to leave. Almost. Her head buzzing from the prospect of spending a night with him again was the only adequate incentive. Thoughts of what they'd be doing were bubbling up in her blood at a much higher intensity than the Roosevelt Bath House's tubs. Fortunately Jake had chosen an in-town location for them to stay the night, only walking distance away from the restaurant. By the time they keyed into the garden level suite of the Saratoga Arms she was as hot as the night air.

"We're all alone," he murmured.

"Convenient, don't you think?"

"Extremely. Anything else you need to say, do it now. You won't be able to speak for a long while after this. I've got much better plans for your mouth."

Man, it's hot in here. Before she could utter a last response, he picked her up and dropped her on the bed with a grin. The lush pillow and mattress he'd placed her on felt like nothing less than a cloud of air. Appropriate, since she felt like she was floating.

Closing her eyes, she blocked out the light that enveloped the room and allowed herself to enjoy nothing but the feel of sensations. The cool air against her skin as he started to undress her.

Until a thought made her tense up. "Would you mind shutting the light off?"

"Actually, I do. You've never given me a chance to see your body," he said, his voice as soft as his touch. "I'm sure your petite figure is as beautiful as your face. I want to see you. All of you."

She shook her head. "Maybe some other time. Can you kill the lights now? Please?"

His brow furrowed. "Talk to me, Ry. What's going on with you?" He gave her a sardonic look. "You really do think I'm ugly."

A small smile spread across her face. "I've already seen you in the buff. You are a very handsome man, Jake Carter." Then her smile faded. "The only person who's unattractive here is me."

"Ryder—"

"I don't want to talk about it." Lifting her head, she kissed him. "There are so many other things we could be doing." To make her point, she gestured toward the zipper of his slacks.

She was shocked when he gently pushed her away. "But—"

"I need you to trust me."

Shit. I have to start getting weepy now*?* "No. Just no. Okay?"

He didn't answer her. His expression looked like he was in pain. Was her defense shield actually hurting him? Driving a wedge between them?

With a move so fast she didn't have time to second-guess herself, she got up to strip. Moments later, she was completely naked. Though her body shook from nerves she stood there for a full ten seconds, her eyes focused on the wall. Then she dive-bombed back into the bed, the blanket wrapped around her tight enough to be a shroud.

A sea of stomach acid stormed inside her. Tentatively she looked at his face to gauge his reaction. His expression, however, remained neutral. "Say something. Damn it!" She swallowed hard and averted her gaze. "Please?"

"Let go of the blanket, Ry."

Biting her lip, she did as he asked. Then she felt him trace the lines of her scars with his fingertip. Softly, gently, as if a mere feather. Her skin flinched at first and then relaxed. Heat soon surged wherever his hand stroked.

Until a thought cooled her down. *He can't possibly be okay with this.*

"Stop making that face," he chastised lightly. "I see your scars. They're not a big deal. To me, anyway. I'm sorry you're so worried about them." He stretched out next to her, lying on his side to face her. "What's it going to take to prove I think you're beautiful?"

She ignored the feel of a single trickle rolling down her cheek. "A trophy. You got one?"

His lips curved upward. "I'll have one ordered right away. I'll even get it engraved for you. *Most Attractive Woman. First Place in Both Head and Heart Categories.*"

Wide-eyed, she stared at him. His words made her heart beat faster.

"Ry, I'm beyond attracted to you. Inside and out. I want to be with you. See where our relationship goes. I can talk to you in ways I can't with any other person. I don't just want you in my bed. I want you in my life." He took her hand and placed it against his lips. "I want to be with you, Ryder. In every possible way."

His other hand traced the outline of her curves, forcing a ripple of pleasure to shimmer through her.

Timidly, she took a hand and traced the outline of his body as he had hers. The cool feel of his skin was in stark contrast to the burning trail he left on her. She opened his button-down shirt. Let her hand glide over his tight abs. Up toward his torso. When she stroked his nipple his eyes closed in apparent bliss.

The fine hairs of his chest felt like downy feathers. The comparison of him to a baby bird almost made her laugh until she stroked a part of him lower down. There was nothing funny about the length and hardness of this gorgeous man, merely awe. A soft groan escaped his lips. "My Lord, Ryder. What you do to me."

What you to do me.

He got up to strip his clothes off, moving faster than one of his racehorses. When he got back into bed he put his hand over hers. "Touch me," he ground out.

"I want to." Reaching down to hold his naked length, she could feel him twitch in anticipation. When she tightened her grip she felt him tighten, too. A drop of slickness smoothed the strokes of her hand motion, which was tantalizingly slow. She relished the pleasure she was giving him.

"You're killing me," he said through gritted teeth. "But if I have to die, this is how I want to go."

"Don't die. You're the one man who could never be replaced."

He looked at her dead-on. "I won't. I'd hate to leave you."

She blinked, melting from his words even more than she had from his acceptance of her body. Or from the searing sexual fire building within.

He moved on top of her and brought his lips down to hers, followed by a trail of kisses down her breasts. Lower and lower until he traced the soft fine hair above her thighs with his fingers. And then with his tongue.

She bit back a cry as her hips bucked. Soon she shattered into a thousand tiny little shards of glass.

Riding high from her orgasm, she barely realized when he pulled away to sheath himself. When he finally did enter her, his long, strong strokes caused her body to combust, his hardness putting her in a blissful haze. A torturous tension built up that cried out for release.

When her second orgasm hit, it finally managed to extinguish the blaze. A moment later, she felt him combust, too.

They lay there together, only moving to wrap their arms around each other. They stayed locked this way, connected in body and in mind.

"I'm not willing to let you go," she said, nuzzling her nose against his chest.

She could admit that now. To him. And to herself.

Chapter 14

Sunlight filtered in underneath the drawn shades of their suite in the Saratoga Arms. Jake held Ryder's body loosely against him as she slept. He'd been awake for quite a while.

The new day had brought him new resolve. Ryder had come a long way in trusting him. Baring her scars was a big step. Even if they were softer after the spa bath. But it wasn't enough.

She was going to have to fight for herself, as well as for her relationship with him. Like he had to fight against his father and people like Barney Smythe. It wasn't only horses that had to win—people did, too. The finish line was more than a physical point, it was mental and even spiritual. The desire to race toward one's ultimate goal, unhindered by doubts and despite any pain. Because doing anything less would be a letdown to one's self.

He was sure Handsome Dancer instinctively knew this. He could only hope Ryder did, too. She was so fragile. Not just physically, with her jockey-esque figure, but with her psyche. For her, it was clearly a much harder blow to be knocked over by people than a mere horse. Some injuries were harder to overcome than others.

He glanced down at the beauty sleeping beside him and watched her eyes flutter open. He squeezed her tighter to him. "Glad you're awake."

She stretched out languidly and gave him a kiss. "Glad to wake up with you."

He pretended to frown. "Then why am I only getting a kiss on the cheek?"

"You know the rule. No toothpaste, no nookie."

"Don't care," he responded, kissing her deeply on the lips until she giggled.

"Let me do you a favor and brush my teeth."

But her attempt to get up was thwarted by his holding her down. "Stop running away. If you really want to do me a favor, you'll ride Handsome Dancer in the upcoming maiden special weight race. Say you agree." He grinned. "You've already got the silks."

Her happy expression faded in front of him. "So much for morning bliss," she groused.

"At least I let you sleep on it."

She rolled her eyes. "I haven't been a jockey for a long time. Assuming I was going to do this, there wouldn't be a whole lot of time for me to get back up to speed. And I have other horses I can't neglect."

"Can Mindy and Lenny help you out more with the others?"

"Lenny already does everything he can for me. Mindy is down a few horses right now, so I can ask her. She's a great trainer but also struggles to get clients."

"I'll make it worth her while if she'll agree to do it."

Ryder bit her lower lip. "I can call her to find out."

Jake felt his heart stop beating. And then flutter with hope. "Does that mean what I think it means?"

He felt her shake and cling tightly to him. Her words were muffled as she buried her head against his bare chest. "I don't know. This is all happening so fast."

He stroked the back of her head, reveling in the softness of her blond hair. "Is it fast? The way your rode Handsome Dancer I could have sworn you were riding him in a race. You can handle him."

"They'll be other horses to contend with on the track. I'm not used to maneuvering through them anymore. Neither is Handsome. It'll be like having two newbies together. At best, we'll lose. At worst, one of us will get injured."

He frowned at the thought. "You know I don't want any harm to come to you. Either of you, actually. But injuries can happen at any time on the track, even if you're the most knowledgeable superstar. You know this field is dangerous. Emanuel knows what he's doing and he still got hurt."

He felt her stiffen next to him. Quickly, he smoothed the back of her hair with his hands to soothe her.

"When my father passed on, Lenny was too happy to teach me to be a trainer. Lenny doesn't have any kids. I think he wants to be sure he can hang on to me. I think that's why he's grouchy all the time. He knows I want to be a jockey again. He's afraid I'll get hurt."

"He's told you not to do it?"

"He hasn't said anything one way or another. He doesn't bring it up and neither do I."

He could swear he felt a drop of water trickle down his chest. He tilted her head up. "Look at me. Are you crying?"

"No. Maybe. A little." She swiped at her eyes. "Lenny's torn. I am, too."

"You've been trained by more than Lenny. You told me your father taught you how to race. You've prepared for years. I doubt you can forget that. For you, it'll literally be getting right back in the saddle."

She said nothing while she traced Jake's chest with a fingertip. He beat the sexual thoughts down and garnered up the strength to finish the important conversation. "Do what's in your heart, Ry. Not for me, not for Lenny, not for Handsome Dancer. Do this for you. You have a golden opportunity. It's the brass ring you've been waiting for. Reach out from the carousel's horse and take it."

He held her chin and her gaze. Her light blue eyes were more beautiful than any he'd ever seen. They reflected sincerity, fear, and hopefulness all at the same time.

"The most injured person around here is me," he quipped. "I've fallen for you hard." He kissed the tip of her nose, wet and salty from her tears.

"My God, Jake . . ." Her voice trailed off.

Good, because I've still got one important thing left to say. "Regardless of what you decide, please know I still want to be with you. I can give up on horses. Business. Even my father. But I can't give up on you."

Her eyes were now round. Large and perfect. He whisked a blond strand away from them.

"Okay," she said softly.

The volume of her voice was so low he thought he might have misheard her. Or that she had said nothing, but he'd heard wishful thinking in the wind. "What did you say?" His own voice was so tight he was amazed his words formed.

She angled herself upward and kissed his lips. "I said okay. I'll do it. I want to make you happy. And maybe it will make me happy." She choked back obvious emotion.

"Do it for you, Ryder. The first person to please is yourself."

"When I'm pleasing you, I'm pleasing me. I'm falling for you, too, Jake Carter."

"Then I promise to be there to catch you. I—" His words were cut off by a sharp beeping from his smartphone.

"You've got to be kidding me," Ryder said sourly. "*Now* your phone has to ring?"

Jake apparently wasn't thrilled by the timing either. He cursed as he leaned over the nightstand to pick it up. But when he glanced at it he smiled. "Oh," he remarked, his voice perky. "Excellent. It's nine o'clock already." He hopped off the bed, grabbed a robe and stealthy opened the suite's door.

What the heck is he doing? "Um, Jake? Everything all right?" Then she watched him bend down and pick up a large box.

"Right on time." He shut the door and practically ran back to the bed. "The package is for you. Open it." He sounded like an enthusiastic child.

Her eyes went wide. "Thank you, but what's the occasion? Christmas in July?"

"Funny. Open it."

She grinned. "Okay. I'm excited." She tore off the bright, multicolored gift-wrap and then lifted up the box's lid.

With delicate fingers, she took out a derby hat, similar to the one she had admired in the store, only this one was decked out in his stable's colors.

He smiled at her, his expression warm and deep. "Whether you're racing my horse or in the stands with me, I want you wearing my colors. I want the whole world to know you're mine."

Her heart soared, her breathing hitched, and her mouth dropped open.

Jake seemed only too happy to kiss her lips closed.

Chapter 15

Back in Long Island, Jake sat at the same French restaurant, at the very same table, he had dined at with Ryder a few weeks ago on their first date. This time, however, with a much less pleasurable companion. His father. The old man looked at him with a grim expression.

It had been a long, hard conversation so far, and the prospect of it getting better was thin. The ordeal had taken a toll on Jake. He had come to the meeting with an open mind, but it was hard not to have his mood grow as dark as the late-evening sky. "I don't know what to tell you, Dad. I hear you. I'm sorry you're upset. But I care about Ryder Hannon. Upsetting her is going to upset me, so you can't call her anymore."

His father straightened in the wooden chair. Jake marveled at the quality of the suit, shirt, and tie his father wore. No matter how much Jake spent to look like a million, his father seemed to actually spend a million. As his father poured himself another glass from their expensive bottle of wine, Jake wondered if he had ever seen his father look casual. Like an actual father instead of a businessman. Even as a child Jake couldn't remember ever seeing him in jeans. A tee shirt. Or, God forbid, sweatpants. *I'll have to ask Dina if she remembers a time when Dad dressed down.*

"Ah, there she is," his father remarked with great enthusiasm.

What? Who is he talking about? Jake was confused until he watched his father gesture over a tall, thin, brunette beauty in a couture knee-length dress. His stomach sank. *Betsy.* His hands clenched into tight fists. *Dad's* got *to be kidding me.* "Dad," Jake ground out. "I don't think you've gotten my message. Stop interfering with my life."

"Nonsense," his father bellowed to the consternation of a couple sitting one table over.

Before Jake could do any more, Betsy was before them. His father ordered the wait staff to bring over another chair. Within seconds, Betsy was seated beside them. With a lovely flush of her perfect cheeks, she lifted an arm to touch Jake's sleeve.

"Don't," Jake warned.

"Where are your manners, son? I invited Betsy to join us for dessert. I was hoping I'd talk some sense into you during dinner. Too bad I didn't get the chance. You were too busy repudiating everything I said. But Betsy here knows I'm a man to be listened to, right?"

Betsy smiled and nodded. "Right you are, Mr. Carter." Then she turned her attention to Jake. "How have you been, Jakey? It's been too long. I've missed you."

Am I on an episode of Punk'd*? Or in a Salvador Dali painting perhaps? If the restaurant's wall clock starts melting to the floor the night still couldn't get any more surreal.* "You miss me because you dumped me. And you did it as soon as you thought I was running low on cash. The horse you asked me to buy was draining my wallet, so you didn't want to waste any more of your time on me. That about right?"

"Jake," his father said in a warning tone.

"It's all right, Mr. Carter," Betsy said. "I expected this. I never did explain to Jake the reason why I left him."

She turned to Jake. "I thought your financial situation was stressing you out so much I couldn't make you happy anymore. I left to give you space." She looked down at the table and caught her breath before she risked eye contact again. "To be honest, Jakey, I also wanted to make things easier on myself. It's hard to be around a man who doesn't notice you anymore." She picked up his hand and held it. "It was a bad call on my part, I know. I should have stuck it out. Somehow I should have convinced you to focus on me. But I ran away instead. I'm so—"

Jake took his hand back and placed it firmly beside him. "It was a terrible call."

"You need to give her a chance," his father commanded. "Instead of being interested in the hired help like your horse trainer, Betsy here is one of *our* kind. Well-bred—"

"Handsome Dancer is well bred, but you didn't like my selection with him. Go figure," Jake quipped.

"Listen to me, Jakey," Betsy pleaded, "I'm not—"

"What you're not," Jake interrupted, "is going to be with me." He pushed out his chair and rose from the table. "Since you two seem to value each other's company so much, feel free to enjoy the rest of the evening together. I've got a date with the hired help. Good night."

With those parting words, Jake walked out of the restaurant.

Ryder swallowed hard and grabbed the doorknob to her office, bracing herself. The room was only partially lit, whatever light there was filtering in through the window. In a few minutes, the sun would be full down. She hit the light switch and called out, "Lenny?"

The old man walked in heavily from a back room. "Ryder? Did you forget something?"

Yes, my courage. "Um, no. I wanted to speak with you."

Lenny rested his rear end on the edge of a desk and crossed his arms over his chest expectantly.

I wonder if that's where I get it from? Geez, the posture looks so self-protective. Defensive, even. "I'm going to come right out and say it. I'd like to . . . no, I need to . . . race again professionally. At least one last time. Jake Carter has asked me to be the jockey for Handsome Dancer, and I said yes." She coughed and felt herself squirm. "I want you to be the official trainer so I'm not playing both roles. Will you do this for me?"

Lenny's eyes popped open but he said nothing for a long while.

"Speak to me, Lenny. Please?"

"I have no problem having you put me down as the trainer. But watching you race is going to kill me, little girl," the old man said, his words dry. "What's going to happen if you fall again? What's going to happen to *me* if I watch you fall again?"

"I know, Lenny," she answered softly. "For a long while, I couldn't bear the thought of it myself. I was hospitalized for a long time, and I'm lucky I didn't get killed."

"Does Jake Carter want that to happen to you?" he shot out defiantly. "'Cause if he does, I've got a right hook he won't be able to duck. I may be old but I can still fight like a man."

"You're fighting for me, Lenny. I get that. I love you for it. My dad loved you for it, too. Mom has always been so happy you take care of me the way you do." She struggled to get words past her own tight throat. "When Dad passed on, I don't know what I would have done without you. You were one of my support pillars, always around so I wouldn't feel alone. Even during my worst days of depression." She walked over to him and hugged him tightly. His gnarled arms wrapped around hers and he kissed her cheek.

"You're my kid, Ryder. You are your dad's kid, too, I know. But you're still mine, nonetheless."

It's the most heart-felt thing he's ever said to me. Probably to anyone. Ever.

He let her go. She took a step back. She'd never seen the tough old man red-eyed before. "I love you, too, Lenny."

He sniffed and shoved a hand in his pocket to take out a handkerchief. He nodded. "Better not let anything happen to you out there. If it does, Jake Carter is going to answer to me."

Chapter 16

The day of the race brought Ryder a new level of nervous energy. Along with a new level of problems. The first was a sealed letter that'd been left on her office chair that morning. The envelope was blank but the inside message had plenty to say with just a few words. *Jake Carter does not date trash.*

She'd swallowed down bile. *Who the heck wrote this?* She'd grabbed the paper, ready to ball it up and throw it into the trash, but she'd thought better of it. If this was harassment of some kind, she might need it for the police. She shoved the message into her desk and out of her mind.

The second problem was even more unbelievable.

"Where's Clem?" Ryder demanded of everyone in her stalls. But no one was able to tell her where the goat had gone. *Of all days for Clem to disappear.* Handsome Dancer had taken to the brown and white goat as if his very own personal pet. The goat had a calming effect on the horse even Ryder herself had a hard time duplicating. When Handsome periodically thrashed in his stall, Clem would hear the racket and bleat loud enough to get Handsome's attention. The horse would lower his head over the stall's door, and Clem would stretch his neck out until they touched. The effect on Handsome would always be immediate. Ryder had joked that Clem worked better than Xanax. *When I find Clem I'm going to touch my head to his, too. If it can work on nervous animals, why not me?*

But after looking high and low, Clem was nowhere to be found. Even the chickens had proverbially flown the coop. "Henrietta Hen? Carly Cluckster?" She called out their silly names but heard no more of them than she had the missing goat.

Handsome Dancer was shifting around nervously in his stall worse than ever, neighing and bobbing his head up and down nonstop. *He needs his friends. How could they all disappear like this?*

She quickly texted Mindy.

Seconds later, Mindy texted back. *Sorry, Ry. Handsome's animal friends must have wandered off. I'd give you a hand rounding them up, but Baby Be Mine is in this race too, and I've got to tend to him.*

Of course Mindy is busy with her own contender. Duh! Ryder gave herself an imaginary smack on the head before texting back, *No problem. Good luck in the race!*

Mindy texted back a smiley emoji with the words, *You, too.*

Ryder was on her own to go find them because the third oddity of the day was Lenny feeling ill. The older man, normally bulletproof from colds and flu, had woken up that morning with a fever. Normally that still wouldn't have kept him away, but the constant vomiting had forced him to stay home. He had been sick enough to warrant her own mother going over there to help him get out of bed.

The only person left of her inner circle was Jake. But as Handsome Dancer's owner, Jake had his own responsibilities to take care of. Like speaking with the Press. Schmoozing up other owners in the VIP area. And promoting not only Handsome Dancer, but all of his horse stock. The bigger the draw his stables got, the more asking money he could potentially get for them. Of course, to help boost his stock's fame, he'd be looking to Ryder to win today's race. Jake was very clear that Handsome Dancer's win would be the centerpiece of his promotional campaign.

She wiped a bead of sweat off her forehead and tried to ignore the blooming headache. The heat and humidity were enough to make her temples throb even without all this added pressure.

Of all the problems, however, the worst by far was the weather. And not just because it was triggering a barometric-pressure-driven headache. A heaviness hung in the air. Oppressive calm right before the storm. The sky was cloudy but still bright enough. The sky's appearance, however, could not be trusted.

Racing during a storm would be her worst-case scenario. A replay of the time she fell, with she and her horse floundering, injured in the mud. Lying face down in torrential rain.

After walking the stalls and their perimeter a half-dozen times, she went back to check on Handsome Dancer. A glance at his pinned-back ears made it clear she wasn't the only one being impacted by the impending storm. His flesh twitched, as if he were electrified by the weather itself.

"Whoa there, Handsome babycakes. We'll get through this." Her voice was as gentle as possible to soothe him. Soft, slow nose rubs helped to calm him down, too. Still, his right hoof kept kicking backward nervously. The horse, usually silent, whinnied persistently.

"Shhhh, it's all right, Handsome Dancer. You'll be back in this stall wearing the blue ribbon way before the storm hits. Clem and Henrietta will be here. You can show them the big basket of victory carrots I'm gonna give you. Then we'll celebrate, warm and dry."

Outside, the wind picked up and the temperature dropped. "Damn. I hope we're going to make it back from the race before the storm hits."

Handsome Dancer peered up at her, his brown eyes soulfully round. *It's as if he can understand me.* "Don't worry, babycakes. I'll be with you the entire way. We will win together." *Or go down together.*

A glance at her watch let her know there was only two hours left before they had to go to the gate.

Handsome whinnied again. He did not sound happy. *Maybe Jake can help calm him down with me.* "I'll be back, soon, Handsome," she said before texting the only ally around to help both her and the horse. When no answer came back, she decided to find him.

Unfortunately, the access to the VIP section was extremely limited. Ryder made her way to the section closest to that area. Frustrating as it was, at least she didn't have to worry about looking out of place among the derby hat wearers in her working-class, denim-clad clothes. There was time enough to change into her jockey silks.

The less she drew attention to herself with the owners' crowd, the happier she was going to be. With her nerves already on-edge she didn't need to hear any unkind comments to throw her confidence further off-kilter. Hopefully the Mets baseball hat she wore would help obscure her face from view. *If I can just grab his attention, we can slip away quick.*

At last she found Jake at the edge of the VIP section on the opposite side from her, near the side-rail. Seeing him was an enormous relief. She exhaled a heavy breath and almost called out to him when she suddenly froze.

The woman standing next to Jake was somehow familiar. Tall and thin with dark brown hair. Ryder squinted to get a clearer look at her. The woman was wearing a derby hat as elegant and expensive as they came. Bows and elaborately painted butterflies danced around a bright green background. The dress she wore had a matching design set against a shiny green fabric that cinched at the waist and flared to the knees.

The overcast sky thankfully prevented the woman from also wearing sunglasses, which would have blocked out her face. But still it was hard for Ryder to tell why she was familiar. Deciding the woman must simply be another owner who hung around the track, Ryder lifted an arm to gesture Jake to come over.

Ryder's arm, however, only got halfway in the air because she saw the brunette smile broadly at a man who also seemed familiar. In fact, the man appeared to be an older version of Jake. Shorter, with thinning hair. *Oh, no, that must be his father. I'd better back away before he sees me.* But Jake's older doppelganger was obviously too engaged with the brunette to notice Ryder.

Ryder turned to leave but stopped when she heard the man loudly say a memorable name. Betsy. *Of course! The woman in the engagement photo.*

Then Jake leaned toward the woman, angled his face under the broad brimmed butterfly hat, and kissed her.

Ryder felt her blood turn to ice. Her heart lurch. A sensation of nausea rise up from her belly until it threatened to spill forth from her already gagging throat.

Jake is a liar.

If there was nothing going on between the two of them, why wouldn't Jake have mentioned he'd be sitting with her in the VIP section? What was he trying to hide? That he had rekindled their relationship? Or that he'd been with her the entire time Ryder and Jake had been together?

Ryder stood there, desperate to hide but with legs firmly bolted to the ground. Her ribcage felt tight, as if it was going to crack. Her breath, and time itself, suspended. After Jake's father put an arm around Betsy, bile reached as far as her teeth. Then the three of them sat down together.

Refusing to run, Ryder crossed her arms over her chest and stared them down. Not that they noticed. *I might as well be invisible.* Her eyes stung. It was a matter of time before her face became as wet as the darkening sky.

Then a thought even more painful hit her. The letter.

Jake Carter doesn't date trash. Did Jake write it? Did the woman? Did Jake's father?

Ryder felt her head spin. Despair swirled and fluttered around her. Maybe Jake didn't care about her after all. Acting out this charade to manipulate her into racing his horse. It's not like anyone else could ride Handsome Dancer. Not with Handsome's temperament and such a short time to get him used to somebody new. Even a more experienced jockey would have a helluva time racing without Handsome's acceptance. Jake even admitted this. Was this why he told her he was no longer involved with Betsy?

The sense someone was staring at her made her look away from Jake and lift her eyes higher in the VIP stands. A man located a few rows up but closer to her side of the stadium gave her a malevolent stare. *Barney Smythe.*

The man shot her a nasty grin. *Figures he's so hostile. His horse is also racing today.* She closed her eyes to remember his horse's name. Knows No something or other. Despite the man's obvious ill-wishes she was about to mouth the words "good luck" to him when she noticed something peculiar on his dark blue blazer. A white and brown feather hanging off the jacket's cuff. Ryder's mouth dropped open, the bile once again threatening to bubble out. *Bastard took Handsome Dancer's pet chicken! He probably has Clem the goat, too. This man will stop at nothing to win.*

Scared for Handsome Dancer's safety, she flew back to the stables as fast as she could go. And then she kept running—far away from both Jake Carter and her ambition to ever jockey again.

Jake sat in the viewing stands with every nerve in his body on edge. *I should be back in the stables seeing if Ry needs a hand.*

He had wanted to make peace with his father, at least as much as possible. Fighting his family was daunting on multiple levels. But more than worrying about being boxed out of business deals, he was worried about being emotionally boxed out.

His father would hopefully come to accept both of them. As long as he and Ryder were together, his father needed to accept them as a couple. His father also needed to understand he was not allowed to quarterback but would be welcomed as a spectator of their winning team.

Jake pulled out his smart phone to send Ryder a text but realized his battery had died. He rolled his eyes in disgust. *Of all days.*

Looking up, he realized his day was going to get worse. Betsy was waltzing her way up and down the VIP viewing stands, her internal GPS obviously on him. She blew him a kiss in what he guessed was her attempt to be sexy. The effort was wasted. Jake felt his expression fall, his happiness break off, hurtling all the way down.

"Great, Dad," Jake whispered to his father, out of Betsy's earshot. "Invite Betsy after I told you I don't want to see her anymore. And more importantly, I told you I'm involved with somebody else."

"Betsy's my guest so be polite."

"I'll be polite to make you happy. I also don't want to cause a scene. But if you don't stop setting me up we're headed for a big fight. I don't want that. I hope you don't either. You don't get to decide how I run my life." There was no choice but to stop talking since Betsy was once more upon them.

"Hi, Jakey." She beamed at him with bright eyes and tilted her head to the side so she could get a kiss.

Biting back his anger at being manipulated, he leaned forward and made a "mwah" sound in the air.

"Let's sit down, shall we?" she said sweetly.

Not to cause a public scene, he did. When she draped a hand casually on his thigh he narrowed his eyes, picked up her hand, and dropped it back on her lap. "Betsy," he said in a low voice with a distinct warning tone. "You need to cut that out. We're not engaged anymore."

She gave him a pout. "I know you're going to change your mind about me. Your father and I have been talking. He knows I want us to get engaged again. I've been trying to talk to you for weeks now." She fluttered long, pretty lashes at him. "I've been jockeying for you, Jakey."

"No, Betsy, you've been jockeying for the best deal around. So long as you think I'm it, that person will be me."

Her mouth dropped open. Her ashen look was almost comical.

"Count me out of your wedding plans, Betsy. This horse has bolted." With that, he stood up. "See you around."

He barely had time to see her face contort in rage as she got up. She ran down the VIP section's central staircase and, in an instant, was gone.

"Son, sit back down. We need to talk," his father said, his words as heavy as lead.

"No, Dad, I'm done with talking. You need to listen."

His father's jaw magically turned into stone. An unmovable statue. "Now see here, I'm tired—"

"I'm tired too, Dad. Tired of you always riding me. You are not my trainer, leading me around until I do your bidding. Nor are you my jockey who can whip me to move faster. I need you to accept me and respect me. And my decisions. Including those about women. I get to decide who I want to be with, not you." Jake paused and cleared his throat. "I know you're only doing what you think is best for me. But it's going to destroy our relationship if you don't back off. I'm a grown man. I need to live my own life."

His father's jaw bounced up and down wordlessly for

a few moments. "Everybody values my advice. Everybody but you. You don't show me any respect."

"Respect doesn't mean total submission, Dad. Respecting you doesn't mean I have to dump my girlfriend because you want me too."

"There is a better woman out there. You made her walk away."

"No. Betsy's not a better woman. You simply think she's better bred. People aren't horses, Dad. And as people, we need to be in control of our own lives. I love you, but you have to let your control issues go."

Jake extended his hand out to his dad, wondering whether he would shake it. "I do love you, Dad. I hope you love me, too. Do you?"

The color drained from his father's face. "Of course I do," he sputtered. "I can't believe you doubt me."

Jake arched an eyebrow. "Good to know. But I'm standing here with my hand in the air, Dad, looking stupid. Are we going to shake or not?"

His father's eyes grew round and his voice quieted. "Before we shake son, I think there's something you need to know."

Jake put his hand down and let out an exasperated sigh. "What?"

"I *might* have left Ryder Hannon a message." His father tugged at his shirt collar uncomfortably.

"You *what*?"

"Okay, I admit it. I left her a note."

"First you call her up and now you're leaving her notes? I can't believe it. Are you going to tell me what your note *might* have said?"

"It's best I go handle the matter myself. Truce?" His father extended his arm for a handshake.

"After you rectify the situation," Jake said flatly, his hands by his sides.

Chapter 17

Ryder sat down on the floor outside Handsome Dancer's stall, tears streaming down her face, not caring about the dirt. The horse was obviously all right. She had done her best with red, swollen, teary eyes to check him out thoroughly. Handsome's mood, on the other hand, was horribly injured. *So is mine.*

With great effort she pulled herself up and peered into his stall. Handsome Dancer stepped forward, one twitching leg at a time. Ryder took hold of his big head and rubbed it in small circles. "It's okay, boy. I'm sad, too. Angry. Hurt. And scared just like you. Wishing I had my friends around me right now."

The horse whinnied softly and settled down. For a moment he closed his large brown eyes. She lifted herself until she touched her nose to his. "Love you, too, babycakes."

When she pulled away, Handsome leaned his head forward to try to nuzzle her. She stroked the white snip on his nose with a gentle hand and blinked hard against stinging tears. Pressure was building up behind her eyes and forehead. Soon she'd have a migraine for sure.

"Because you're one of my friends, Handsome Dancer, I'm going to tell you something. I'm not going to race you today. I'm not in a proper mindset to do it, and I would never jeopardize your safety." She paused and croaked out her next words. "I'm not going to train you after today, either. Because my dealing with Jake Carter is not safe for me." She swallowed hard. "Lord, I need to keep myself safe," she whispered.

"Safe from what?" a familiar voice asked.

Ryder whirled around to see Mindy standing there. Her friend's head was cocked to one side as if trying to evaluate. "I came by to check on the goat situation. Baby Be Mine is already with his jockey, so I figured I'd give you a hand if you needed it. Hey, are you all right?"

"No." It was all Ryder could do not to laugh hysterically. "Not at all."

"Well pull yourself together. This is your big day. Not just Handsome Dancer's, but yours. The rest of the jockeys are either getting their silks on or meeting their mounts. It's time for you to do the same." Mindy's face lit up. "I know you're going to win, Ryder. I did my best for Baby Be Mine, but there's no way you and Handsome Dancer aren't going to take the top prize. I've seen you two in action. You are more than simply horse and rider. You guys are like musical harmony, separate components of one beautiful song. And when you make it to the finish line first, I'll be the first one to sing both your praises."

The words wrapped around Ryder's heart, touching it deeply. "Those words mean a lot to me, Mindy. But I'm not going to ride. I was going to, but then I saw Jake kissing a woman he was engaged to. *Is* engaged to, I think. And his father called me a while back telling me to back away from his son." Her eyes narrowed. "He told me I was too low-brow to be with Jake."

Mindy's eyes widened. "Why that rotten little piece of sh—"

"I know," Ryder agreed. "But he's not the only one. Someone else left me an anonymous note saying Jake Carter does not date trash. It's probably from Jake's father, but who knows? And then there's Barney Smythe. He's the one who stole Clem the goat and the chickens, I'm sure of it." Ryder laughed tightly. "I've got to hand it to him. He did his best to throw Handsome Dancer and me off our game. Worst thing is—it worked. All of it worked. I'm not riding this race. Or any race. I'm never going to be a jockey again."

Mindy's eyes softened but her expression stayed firm. "I understand what they've all done to you is terrible. Though I'm still hopeful Jake has a solid explanation. But even if he doesn't, I don't understand why you're willing to let him and the rest of those idiots win."

Ryder's jaw dropped again. "You don't? You've got to be kidding me."

Mindy breathed in so deeply Ryder could see her chest rise up. "No, I'm not. I think you're kidding yourself. You're afraid, Ry. Scared to take the big chance and fail again. All of these things happening to you is bad, I get that. But they're still excuses. You're looking for reasons to not put yourself out there."

"But—"

"No *buts*, Ry. Unless you're referring to the butt-kicking I'm going to give you. You need a kick in the ass to get you going. No different from when you kick a horse's hindquarters to nudge it along."

Ryder stared at her silently and sullenly, her arms crossed tightly over her chest.

"The truth is," Mindy plowed forward, "whether or not Jake Carter is a two-timing lowlife, he still gave you this opportunity. This golden opportunity to do what other owners would not let you do—to race once again. To live out your dream. Win or lose, you'd be living up to the name your father gave you by trying your best. Don't you want to live out the life, the destiny you deserve?"

Ryder's unfocused gaze found the ground and her hand moved of its own volition to absently stroke Handsome Dancer's mane.

"Look at me, Ry. It's not about any of them. It's about you."

"It doesn't feel like it's about me."

"It will when you get on the horse. Isn't that right, Lenny?"

Out of nowhere, Lenny appeared.

"I saw you coming down the corridor," Mindy chastised. "You can walk softly all you want, but you're not going to sneak up on me again."

Lenny puffed out his chest. "You just finished telling Ryder this is all about her. So why are we talking about you?"

"Or you," Mindy retorted.

"I thought you were sick," Ryder cut in.

"I'm feeling better. I had to be here for you," he answered.

"So what do you think, Lenny?" Mindy asked. "Can we agree on anything? On the one thing that matters? I want Ryder to race today. Do you agree?"

Lenny face scrunched up as he turned toward Ryder. "I hate to admit it, but Mindy's right." He coughed loudly. Whether to clear his throat or eat his words she didn't know. "It's not easy for me to say that," he said, admitting the obvious.

Mindy burst out laughing. "That I believe!"

Lenny ignored the interruption. "It's hard for me because I don't want to see you get hurt. Neither does your mom. She couldn't bear to watch you today. You've been through so much already. Getting injured the last time you jockeyed. Losing your dad. Having to start over. Giving up your racing dream . . ."

"But that's my point, Lenny," Mindy cut in. "She doesn't need to give up on her racing dream. Now's her big chance!"

For once, Lenny was quiet. Ryder watched the old man suck in his lips and lean the weight of his body against a stable wall. "You're all I have, Ryder." Lenny's rough voice shook with emotion. "I want what's best for you, but if something bad happens . . ."

"Nothing's going to happen to her," Mindy protested.

Lenny shot Mindy a withering stare. "Fine for you to say. It's not you who will feel the pain."

"You think I'm not going to feel pain if she gets hurt, old man? If that's what you think, you're even crazier than I thought."

Ryder cut them off before they went another round. "You're both right. It is about me. I need to decide what I really want out of life. Do I want to play it safe? Or bet it all?"

And just like that, the truth she had buried down deep was now unearthed. Her path found. The direction of her footsteps clear. She reached for Handsome Dancer's reins. "Come on, boy. Let's ride."

Jake stopped his father from leaving to demand an answer. "I can't believe you left a note like that for Ryder. What were you thinking?"

His father sat there stiff and mute, barely indicating he heard the words at all. Until Jake noticed the smallest downturn of a lip. Otherwise, Jake would have sworn his father had gone deaf.

"First off," Jake continued, "she's a licensed, professional horse trainer. That does not make her the *hired help*. Second off, even if she did fit that description, I wouldn't care. This is the twenty-first century for crying out loud. There are no social caste systems anymore."

"Are you blind? Of course there are."

Jake twisted his lips into a frown. "Elitist, much?"

At that, his father's right eye twitched. A telltale sign he was pissed.

Good. At least he heard me. "We spoke at the restaurant, Dad. I explained to you I don't want you to interfere. You've overstepped the bounds in a big way. I thought I'd been very clear. And yet you go ahead and do something like this. Something that could destroy me both professionally and personally. And this is on top of you trying to shove Betsy down my throat *again*." Jake shook his head in disgust. "I'd say we'll talk about this later but there's no point. I doubt I'll ever get through to you." He got up to leave.

"Wait, son."

"Sorry, Dad. I've listened to you long enough. The person I've got be with now is Ryder."

As soon as Jake left the VIP section he bumped into his sister and brother-in-law at the bottom of the staircase.

Dina, decked out in some obviously pricey outfit and crazy large derby hat, sighed with relief. "Oh, there you are," she exclaimed. "I just ran into Betsy."

Steven rolled his eyes at his wife. "Why do you have to go there?"

Not answering her husband or missing a beat, Dina slipped her arm around Jake's and tried to steer her brother in the opposite direction. "Ignore my husband. I think you and Betsy should get back together, even if Steven doesn't. Your break-up with her is all because of a silly misunderstanding. You two make the perfect couple."

"Sorry," Steven mouthed wordlessly over Dina's head. "I tried, bro."

If Jake hadn't been so angry he would have laughed. "For God's sakes, Dina, I just went through this with Dad. I want to be with Ryder Hannon. Accept it. Or don't. I'm good either way. Now if you'll excuse me, I've got to go find her."

"Ryder Hannon?" Dina's eyebrows knit together. "Really? The hired help?"

Jake stopped mid-stride and turned around. "Care to say that to me again? This time to my face?" His words were cold steel.

"No, she doesn't." Steven turned to his wife and placed a firm hand on her shoulder. "Let's take our seats now, Dina, and let Jake run his own life."

"But—"

"*Now.*"

Dina's eyes went wide. "All right," she said softly. "I guess I said too much."

"Yes, you did," her husband replied, his voice low and firm. "You and your father need to stop being so controlling. Not just with Jake, either. I'm talking about me, too. I'm not going to build an addition on our house . . ."

Steven's voice grew fainter as Jake turned back around to look for Ryder. With any luck, he'd find her soon. *Oh, Ryder, I'm so sorry.*

He was nearly back at the stalls when he ran into someone else determined to talk. Barney Smythe held his hand out in a signal for Jake to stop.

"Sorry, Barney, I can't stop now. I'll catch up with you after the race. Good luck with Knows No Bounds."

Barney tugged Jake's sports jacket. "I don't need luck. I need to be made whole. You owe me, Jake Carter, and I mean to collect."

Jake took hold of Barney's hand and shoved it off his jacket. "Don't put your hands on me. I don't know what you're talking about, Barney, but now is not the time. Sorry—"

Barney's voice came out in a low growl. "You'd better make the time. Or you're going to *be* sorry."

"What the hell are you talking about? It sounds like a threat, but you make no sense at all."

"I'm talking about Handsome Dancer. You took him from me for a song. You hid his true potential and that's not fair. Now everybody says Handsome Dancer's going to win this race and a whole bunch more races thereafter. I want a share of those winnings."

"I paid you for the horse. The full amount of what you asked. It's not my problem if what you asked is way less than what he's worth. It's your job to know the value of your horses, not mine."

"I don't care! You took advantage of me. So listen up, you're going to give me ten percent of the winnings for this race and the rest of all his wins for the next year."

Jake narrowed his eyes, doing his best to keep his clenched fists at his sides. "Is this some sort of screwed up attempt at racketeering? Why would I agree to this? Am I drunk in your opinion, or just stupid?"

Barney gave a malevolent grin. "Maybe you're both, but I do know you're desperate."

"Interesting you know more about my life than I do." His fists were itching now to make contact with Barney's face.

"I do know more than you, Carter. I know your horse is going to lose unless you agree to pay me my fair share."

Jake stiffened and felt the blood in his veins turn to ice. "Are you planning to hurt Handsome Dancer? If you so much as touch a hair on his bo—"

"Nope. I'd never hurt our *mutual* investment. But I will cause him to lose this race."

"Damn it, Barney, say your piece so I can move on."

"I—literally—have got his goat." Barney laughed. "The damned goat and the rest of his little animal friends are with me."

"Are you crazy, Barney? You're really so nuts you've actually kidnapped a goat? I don't know whether to take this seriously or not. Get the hell out of my way."

"Okay," Barney said breezily. "No problem. I've got other incentives that will make you see things my way."

"Like what?" Jake laughed. "You're going to steal every goat in America to ensure Handsome Dancer never gets another friend? No, that would be silly. You'd have to steal every chicken in the U.S.A. That would be hard to pull off, wouldn't it? So why don't you go ahead and go *pluck* yourself, Smythe." Jake gave a tight smile in an attempt to piss him off more.

Barney's gaze narrowed. "How about more interference with your jockey?"

"What? Are you saying you're responsible for Emanuel's fall? That would be a crime you're admitting to . . ." He felt his body freeze, slowly turning to ice. "Are you saying you're going to hurt Ryder? You son of a bi—"

"Define *hurt*." Barney's grin was a long, slow snake. "A letter from your father telling her to back away from you and calling her trash might affect her ability to ride. It's hard to compete properly and safely when you're in a bad frame of mind. I was happy to deliver your father's messages to her."

"You're a lying sack of shit, Smythe. Why would I listen to you?"

"Because I owe your father a lot of money. If my horse comes in, I can at least afford to pay him off and get him off my back. Why do you think your father hates your girlfriend so much? Leaving her nasty messages? Your dad wants Knows No Bounds to win as badly as I do so I can pay him back. Handsome Dancer is the only real challenge to my horse right now. But if I get a share of Handsome Dancer's future earnings, I'll have enough to pay him back and still keep some."

"You owe my father money?" Jake felt like he'd been slapped in the face. "How is that possible?"

"You think of your father as Mr. Perfect, don't you? The elegant, all-righteous businessman. What a fool you are. Your father is not what he seems. Sure, he's got legitimate businesses but he's also a loan shark. *My* loan shark. It's not only the racetrack that makes money off of horse betters. Your father does, too. And he makes his money on me because I gamble. A lot."

"You're crazy. I would know if my father was a loan shark."

"Would you? I'm guessing he controls how much of him you really get to see." Barney suddenly shifted his gaze around the area. Sweat broke on the man's brow. The weather, albeit warm, was not hot enough to generate that kind of reaction on its own.

"You'd be surprised how much power your father has," Barney persisted. "His secret is well kept. He likes it that way. No one wants to cross him. Including me. So I need to pay the bastard off. Answer me, Jake, are you in?"

"Am I in? In what?"

"Are you going to give me a cut of Handsome Dancer's winnings or not?"

Jake stood there, contemplating whether to deck the man in the face or call the cops.

"Jake, what's it going to be? You need to answer me now. Are you in? Or does something bad need to happen that will make you wish you paid me off?"

Chapter 18

"Wait, Ryder," Lenny called out.

Ryder dropped Handsome Dancer's reins and turned around to see the old man fidget more nervously than she had ever seen him. "Yes?"

"I want to say something to you." Lenny twisted his hands together, seemingly unconscious he was doing so. His eyes scanned the stables, no doubt double-checking Mindy had truly gone.

"Okay." Ryder touched Lenny's shoulder. "I'm listening."

"I never thought I'd say this, but Mindy's right. You should race. You need to race. And I need to support you. Having you do what's best for me isn't fair. I'm an old man. You have your whole life ahead of you. It's time for you to do what's best for you." He gulped hard, his eyes downcast. "I'm sorry, Ry. I let you down."

"No, you didn't."

"I did, but you don't understand the full reason why. I had to suffer watching you in the hospital, and then at home, healing from your cracked ribs, your skin tears, and your concussion. You were in so much pain. I was in so much pain seeing you like that."

Oh my God, is Lenny getting teary again?

"I felt guilty. Your father did, too. Maybe we pushed you too hard into racing. And now it's become part of your blood. Like it's in mine."

"I chose this, Lenny. Nobody forced me. When I quit racing to become a trainer you supported me every step of the way. You're always there when I need you. Whatever my goals have been you've done your best to make me successful. Don't blame yourself." She leaned over to kiss his cheek. The feel of his thick beard tickled her skin.

Then his arms suddenly wrapped around her shoulders and drew her in for a tight hug.

Her eyes widened in surprise. She wrapped her arms around him and shut her eyes tight. "Love you, Lenny."

"I know, honey, I know. Now enough of this mushy stuff before Mindy comes back and sees us. I couldn't live it down."

Laughing, Ryder let him go. "Right. I'd hate for you to ruin your reputation as a curmudgeon."

The corners of Lenny's lips rose into an unheard of configuration—a smile. "No, I certainly wouldn't want that. Now go change into your silks. You've got a race to win, Ms. Jockey."

With a grateful smile, she walked back to her office to change. Normally a jockey would have a valet set out all the needed equipment, from riding silks to helmet, but she was on her own. Knowing that, she had already gathered everything she'd need.

After putting on her riding pants and boots, she snaked her arms through the jockey jacket then grabbed a bunch of goggles in case it rained. The goggles would go over the top of her helmet, the only weather protection she'd have.

She was already outside when she remembered to grab a saddle. A quick detour put the lightweight saddle in her hands. It weighed only a few pounds, a contraption that almost defied common sense to sit in. The harness was hardly better, merely some lightweight leather straps that included a bit for the horse's mouth. If a car had such inconsequential steering equipment, a lot more people would die driving.

Unfortunately, lightweight equipment was a necessary evil. In moments she'd be weighed by the racetrack officials along with the rest of the other jockeys. The total weight allowed, including saddle weight and all other equipment, was capped at 126 pounds. She wasn't too worried about the cap. Plus, nerves had kept her from eating too much this last week anyway. If anything, they'd probably find her underweight. If they did, she'd have to add equipment for poundage.

Then she remembered the rich chocolate cake Jake spoon-fed her last night, right before he'd placed the chocolate elsewhere . . . She shook off the now-painful memory and headed to the bathroom. *Maybe I can pee out some water weight.*

In the bathroom, she caught a glimpse of herself in the mirror. The last time she had seen herself look like a jockey was the afternoon of the fall, several years ago. The thought almost made her change back into her trainer's clothes. *Maybe it is better to try and fail than to not try at all. Wouldn't the bigger failure be never giving myself the chance to succeed?*

She noticed her reflection bore the same odd countenance as Lenny. A smile. *I am doing this. Not for Jake Carter. Not to prove a point to anyone else. I am doing this for me.* She tightened the straps on her helmet and walked off to be weighed.

I really am a jockey again. Just like you, Dad. The Ryder you always wanted. And the rider I need to be.

Jake checked the stalls to find both Ryder and Handsome Dancer gone. *I'm too late.* He could only hope Handsome Dancer was willing to run, given the loss of his animal friends and his jockey undoubtedly in a bad mood. Neither horse nor rider would be at their best with such drama surrounding them.

Worse, the sky was darkening at a fast pace. Gray clouds

drifted together as if magnetized. The little bit of blue sky left was ebbing away.

The tempo of Jake's heartbeat was gaining a momentum as rapid as the clouds. If he didn't calm himself down, he would be of no use to anyone.

It was wise to stop and think about the best course of action. Checking in on Ryder wasn't feasible anymore. Barney's bullshit had made Jake miss her. In moments she'd be parading Handsome Dancer out onto the track with all the other contenders. They'd walk out, giving bettors their chance for a last-minute inspection and bets, and then line up to the gate. A silent plea for her safety was the best he could do at this point.

If the rain broke while Ryder was on the track, the risk of injury would dramatically go up. Not only did mud make a lot of horses skittish, it made for slick conditions. Worse, any horse not in the lead would suffer from having mud thrown in its face. The same mud would also be thrown into the jockey's face, dangerously impairing vision. Goggles often could not withstand the assault for too long and even having back-up goggles could fail, creating a dangerous racetrack filled with jockeys riding some of the fastest, biggest, most powerful animals on earth. Trying desperately to not crash into each other.

If they failed, or a horse simply stumbled on its own, both jockey and horse could be horribly injured or even trampled to death. Exactly like what had happened to Ryder last time she rode.

I can stand suffering a lost race. But I can't stand losing her.

"Jake?" said a voice from behind him.

Hmm, what? He spun around. "Dina? I told you, I'm through discussing— Hey, are you okay?" He squinted as his sister came closer. Her eyes were red-rimmed and swollen. He frowned. "Where's Steven? Does he know you're upset?"

"Sure he knows. He's upset, too. Right now he's yelling at Dad. I left to come find you."

He shook his head. "No, sorry, I can't. You'll need to tell me later. I've got to get a message to Ryder. I don't want her racing in these conditions. Handsome Dancer is already skittish to begin with. The rain is only going to compound the problem."

"That's what I came to talk to you about, Handsome Dancer. I overheard Dad fighting with Barney Smythe." Dina let out a whimper. "Dad assured Barney that Handsome Dancer couldn't possibly win. Apparently Dad not only bet on Barney's horse, but he tried to fix this race, too." Dina let out a strangled cry. "I can't believe it. Why would Daddy do such a thing?"

"I can't answer that."

Dina blinked in surprise. "You knew about this, didn't you?"

"I found out a few minutes ago. Barney told me. He said if I didn't give him a cut of Handsome Dancer's winnings, he'd see to it his horse won. He blamed the whole thing on Dad, calling him a loan shark. Barney said he owed Dad money."

"I can't believe it."

Jake arched a single eyebrow. "Can't you?"

Dina looked at him soulfully.

"I wouldn't be surprised if he did. You've always bought into all his crap, Dina. I know you're better than all that stuff of his you spout. Telling me I need to be dating only *pedigree* people. And that Steven has to work his butt off to afford things like an unnecessary addition to your house. If Dad wasn't so obsessed by money maybe he wouldn't be loansharking in the first place. His legit business ventures have generated more than enough cash. I think people who can't be happy with what they have, have a problem. Don't you?" He gave her a pointed look.

"Maybe Dad is obsessed with money," she said. "Maybe I am, too."

All of a sudden the rain came. From light drops to heavy ones in almost an instant. Quickly turning into hard slats of pummeling rain.

Jake tensed. *"Did you need to tell me anything else? Because I've got to go."*

Dina seemed not to notice the oncoming downpour. She grabbed ahold of Jake and drew him near her. "I love you, little brother." Her voice was gravely as if she were going to sob again. "At least we have each other. I heard what you said and promise to be a better sister to you." Her lips pressed together tightly in a thin line before adding, "Sounds like I need to be a better wife to Steven, too."

"Steven loves you. I love you. Don't worry, Dina. We'll get through whatever issues with Dad. Now you've got to go, and so do I."

"Thanks, Jake. Good luck with the race. And good luck with Ryder, too. If she's the woman you want, I'm happy to welcome her." She gave him a timid smile and then sprinted away, hand on her large hat as she fought through the wind and rain to get back to her husband.

As Jake hurried on, the track's huge digital billboard caught his eye. The new message downgraded the condition from 'fair' to 'poor.' Soon it would read 'sloppy.' With each downgrade, Ryder would be in more danger.

He searched for an official to pull her out. He'd just gotten hold of someone when "sloppy" appeared in large white digital letters.

Shit!

And then Jake heard the sound of the bugle start the race. *Oh, God, Ryder.* His heart sank and his stomach tensed. Helpless, he walked away to stand in the downpour to watch.

He'd be damned if he admitted it was more than rain causing the water in his eyes.

Chapter 19

Ryder sat in the number one gate, placed approximately six furloughs from the finish line, her jaw set tight. Horses typically hated this gate, the one closest to the inside rail. This gate would get the first horse loaded, leaving that horse antsy while waiting for the rest of the horses to be put into their own gates. A restless horse was one that could thrash about and hurt itself or the jockey. It would also force the horse to start off against the rail, which could sometimes cause it to become trapped. A gate further down would allow better manipulation to get into the lead, and then edge toward the inside for a faster route to the finish line.

Handsome Dancer was agitated today to begin with. Getting stuck with the one gate wasn't going to help. But which gate a horse got was the luck of the draw. A gamble, like the rest of horseracing. She could only hope the rest of this race would get better.

"Easy, babycakes, take it easy." She stroked his mane and spoke softly to him. "We're going to get through this, you and me."

As if Mother Nature wanted to prove her wrong, the sky opened up with a *crack*. Then the wind picked up, starting slow but working its way into a howl. A few big heavy drops splashed against her skin. Handsome Dancer's ears went flat and his flesh twitched. With a rough snort, he pawed at the ground with his front right hoof.

Suddenly more rain came with a strength that pummeled her. It stung her skin as it came in sideways sheets. *Lord, it's my worst nightmare.*

And then she wasn't on Handsome Dancer anymore. No, in her mind she was on Makin' Waves, the horse of her *last* race. Her father was not only alive but watching her from the viewing stands. Makin' Waves' owner stood by her father's side. The owner's face was calm and cool. Her father, however, gripped his hat tightly in his hands, a grimace on his face. No matter how much he believed in her, the risk of injury was too high for a parent to ignore. Her mother, also supportive, couldn't bear to watch at all. "Maybe I'll get braver as time goes on," her mother had said. Ryder had laughed off their concern. *Parents worry so much. But at least mine encourage me to do what I was born to do.*

Ryder, in her mind's eye, saw her father's face as Makin' Waves bolted from the gate and took off in the lead. Only to fall midway through and crash down onto her.

She closed her eyes as she remembered the feeling of wet earth cutting into her skin. And then the tremendous *boom* as Makin' Waves fell on top of her. Then nothing as the world stood still. No noise. No vision. Nothing. Until the world had started up again at a speed high enough to generate cyclones. Everything, sound, vision, crashing down on her at once. Along with the pain. The deep searing pain. It shot through her neck, back, and legs. Then she felt it in the ribs before everything went black.

She hadn't actually seen her dad's face when she fell. Even if she had wanted to look for him, he would have been indiscernible in the distance through the crowds. Yet she pictured him now, his face morphing, twisting in an agony that mirrored her own.

Handsome Dancer bucked underneath her, dragging Ryder into the here and now. She felt her chest expand and contract quickly as if struggling to get air. *Now is not the time for a panic attack.*

"The horses are all loaded," she heard somebody behind the posts shout out. "Get ready!"

Ryder shoved her goggles over her eyes, with more ready to drop down if needed. Then the gate doors opened and Handsome Dancer leapt out. He took off like a thunderbolt, seemingly oblivious to what the other horses were doing.

Ryder kept her position more upright, steering Handsome Dancer through the dangerous crowd. A storm of dark, beautiful bodies thundered along at shockingly high speeds. The mud kicked back from the horses' hooves, cutting into their skin and blinding them. Within moments, her first pair of goggles became ruined, the lenses scratched and clouded from the sharp mud. She pulled down her second pair. *Damn. At this pace, I'll have gone through my last pair before ever hitting the finish line.*

Handsome kept his head low to avoid the muddy onslaught. But if she didn't bring it up, the weight of his hanging head would slow him down and make them lose. *I've got to get us out of here.*

She started steering Handsome through the throng to bring him closer to the outside, leaving the inside rail far behind. The sound of the horses' hooves thundered loudly in her ears. Weaving Handsome Dancer though the herd was no easy task. It required spotting the minutest holes to shove through. Too tight a fit could lead to bumping, which would disqualify them. Or ban her from being able to ride. Or worst of all, result in a crash. *Am I crazy? Why am I worried about being able to race again when I haven't even survived this one?* Her hands grasped Handsome Dancer's reins so tightly the skin around her knuckles threatened to crack.

With a final bob and weave, she and Handsome made it all the way to the outside. They were well past the fourth furlough, getting closer to the home stretch. Time for a tactical choice. Should she conserve his energy a little longer or tell Handsome to go for it, hoping he had enough strength to keep up his highest speed until they reached the finish line, two furloughs away? *No, I'm through with playing it safe. In racing, and in life. I'm here to win, not just make do.*

She grit her teeth, her body tense with resolve. She spurred him on faster, bent her knees until her butt hovered right above the saddle, and then leaned her upper body forward to spur the horse on. As Handsome gained stride she shoved her second pair of ruined goggles down around her neck and reached over her helmet to bring down the last pair.

The eighth pole, marking the fifth furlough, appeared. *I'm going to go for broke. It's show time.*

She leaned further forward in the saddle. "Let's go!"

Handsome bolted. Suddenly, they were flying down the track. *He wants this. Handsome Dancer wants to win. And now I know I want this, too.*

In seconds they were a full length ahead of the pack. Ryder reached up and held on to Handsome's neck, dropping the reins completely. "Keep your head up, boy," she called out. Instantly she felt his head steady once again and his body surge forward.

They were almost two full lengths ahead. *Almost there!*

The wind howled around them, heightened by their great speed. The rain crashed down in torrents, impossible to see. They surged forward, a single creature going for victory. One heart. One mind. One goal.

Feeling an empty, painful pit in his stomach, Jake cursed as he made his way back toward the viewing stands. *I should have stopped her. If anything happens to her, it's my fault.*

Win or lose he was going to be there for her. All that mattered was that she made it back safe to the finish line. *I'm the one who pushed her into this dangerous situation. What was I thinking?*

The drama of the day had made it clear there was only

one person who needed to be the focus of his life. A woman who would forever be in the winner's circle. At the center of his life. His whole world.

A smile crept up his face. *There's no fighting it. No denying it. I am in love with Ryder.*

But with that realization came pain. *If anything happens to her . . .* Jake clutched at a handkerchief in his pocket, balling it up and kneading it in between his fingers with nervous energy. His face twisted around painfully though he hardly noticed it.

He felt a gentle arm on his shoulder and turned around to see his sister. Dina gave him a warm smile. "She'll be okay, Jake. She might even win."

Jake nodded, too focused on the unfolding race to verbally acknowledge his sister's words.

"Holy crap, bro," Steven marveled, his attention focused exclusively on the track. "I think she's going to win."

It was hard to see in the downpour. "What?" He swallowed and tried to breathe.

The announcer's voice, crackly and hard to distinguish through the sound of the heavy rain, filled the air.

"Handsome Dancer is in the home stretch, folks. He's being ridden today by Ryder Hannon, daughter of the legendary late Phil Hannon. This is Ryder Hannon's first time back in the jockey's saddle after years of retirement. And riding she is, folks! Handsome Dancer is in the clear lead. He's more than two lengths ahead of Tex Arkana right now, who's in second place. Knows No Bounds is in third place, with Baby Be Mine following close behind. Now Baby Be Mine moves up to third place with Tex Arkana still in second place. But Handsome Dancer is staying in the lead. This is it, folks, they are coming to the finish line. Handsome . . ."

And then the voice of the announcer was lost as a crack of lightning filled the air. The loudspeaker glitched, letting out a loud buzz.

And for a split-second, Jake felt his heart glitch out, too.

Ryder didn't even hear the announcer's voice proclaiming their victory. Or the shouts and cheers from the few spectators who stuck it out to the end. She only saw her and Handsome Dancer cross the finish line. Felt the two of them slowing down as they passed it. Only then did she feel her heart start beating again. They had done it. They had won. Tears rolled off her cheeks, blending in with the rain.

"Oh my God, my big Handsome babycakes. We did it." Her voice was so soft no doubt the horse didn't hear her words. But he understood her anyway, she was sure of it. She patted the horse to slow him down even more and bent forward to kiss his sopping wet neck. "Yup, we did it, boy. You are a real winner. The winner I knew you were all along."

She went around the track with Handsome Dancer until he cooled down a bit and then rode him to the winner's circle. When they made it there, she stopped and dismounted, practically blind from the rain. With a firm hand, she pulled the dirty goggles down around her neck and blinked to clear her eyes.

The rain was getting lighter. A small ray of sunlight could be seen in the distance, creeping in through the clouds. Enjoying a minute of perfect happiness, she smiled. Until she saw Jake.

His skin was pale and his clothes soaked, just like hers. In fact, she noticed he was shivering. Whether from cold or nerves she didn't know. It didn't matter. Jake's expression was warm. Without a word, he stepped forward and opened his arms.

She froze. "I thought you were with your fiancée," she said in a voice barely louder than a whisper.

"I *am* with my fiancée."

Ryder's heart sank. Her eyes stung, more than they had from the mud and the barrage of rain. It didn't matter if her eyes hurt, she didn't want to see him and the brunette anyway. She turned around to walk away, but he put an arm around her.

"I thought you'd be more excited about the engagement."

"Thrilled," she shot out bitterly. "I hope the two of you will be very happy."

He blinked in surprise, and then let loose a large grin. "What are you talking about, Ry? I meant *you*. The two of us. I want you to be my wife, Ryder Hannon. I love you. I want to be with you forever." He dropped down on one knee, onto the wet concrete floor, in front of a small crowd that now stood in stunned silence. "Will you marry me?"

Speechless, she nodded, until she got her voice back. *He was right. I should have learned to trust him.* "Yes. I love you, too, Jake Carter. I know I always will."

What the people around her were saying or doing after that she didn't know and didn't care. Until she became aware of the announcer's voice coming through loud and clear over the racetrack's loudspeakers, once again working.

"Ladies and gentlemen, Ryder Hannon just said yes to horse owner Jake Carter's marriage proposal. Looks like she not only won first place but won love, too. It's a happy day at Belmont Park."

"I will always love you, Ryder," Jake whispered in her ear.

Epilogue

Four years later

Ryder walked into the library room of their enormous house as quietly as she could. *Should I sneak up on him and declare victory? Or let him think he won?* She debated how much she should tease her little son for a moment before caving in. "Okay, okay, I give up," she called out in a singsong voice. "Where are you, Lenny Philip Carter? Come out, come out, wherever you are!"

Her three-year-old boy giggled loudly, giving his "secret" location away. Then he popped out from behind the leather couch. "Here I am!" He grinned broadly at her, his dark hair flopping in his face.

My son may be named after Lenny, but he's the spitting image of Jake.

Little Lenny put his hands on his hips and stuck his chin out. "I knew you wouldn't be able to find me. I always know what to do."

Ah, now that's more like how Lenny was. Ryder's eyes welled up with emotion thinking of the old man. He had lived a long, healthy life until his massive heart attack. The only upside was he didn't suffer a long illness and had had no mental decline. He had left the world as he had lived in it, strong and outspoken. The one milestone change of his life had been his attitude toward Mindy. Lenny had come around to be as fond of her as Ryder was. On most days, anyway, when they weren't fighting. Mindy hadn't entirely given up bear baiting the old man. She had insisted her teasing kept him young.

Ryder bit back a smile. As much as Lenny had denounced Mindy, deep down he loved all the attention. For a man who had been afraid to be left alone in his old age, he had been showered with attention from two women he cared about deeply.

Still, the pain of missing him would always be there. She could no more forget about him than she could her own father.

"Momma, are you crying?"

"No."

"But a tear is rolling down your face."

Ryder gave a hard swipe at her eyes. "Must be all the dust in here."

"There's no dust," Little Lenny protested. "The housekeepers are here every day."

The kid's as stubborn as Lenny, too. She suppressed a laugh. "Then maybe these are tears of joy from finding you after my long, hard search."

Little Lenny puffed his chest out proudly.

"Yup, you're a tricky one," Ryder continued. "Although maybe next time you should pick a different room to hide in. You're always in the library."

"But I like this room," Little Lenny insisted. "It's got all your trophies."

He gestured over to a wood and glass cabinet Jake specially built to showcase all her victories. The cabinet was oversized to accommodate trophies that were quite large. But of them all, there was one award treasured beyond the rest. A large silver urn supported by a base of tiny thoroughbred horses. One of the horseracing world's most coveted winner's cups, and it was all hers. It seemed like seconds, not years, since Handsome Dancer had won it for the longest, most difficult, and most respected American thoroughbred race, the Belmont Stakes. The day the New York Racing Association handed it to her, Jake and Big Lenny—jockey, owner, and trainer—had been one of the best days of all three of their lives.

Although Jake joked their wedding hadn't been too bad, either. Small and offshore, they avoided the paparazzi that would have surely happened given the controversy surrounding his father's questionable business dealings. They were glad the fallout hadn't hurt Jake's success or overall reputation. Jake established the Jacob and Ryder Carter Charitable Foundation, which funded programs to help problem gamblers refrain and hopefully reform. Fewer problem gamblers in the world would mean less prey for loan sharks.

The family crisis had brought about one good result. Dina had reformed her own ways quite a bit. The result was better relationships with not only her husband but Jake and Ryder, too.

Ryder had more time to spend with family now. She still ran her training business but had quite a few people helping her out. With Mindy being the lead. Jake and Ryder had offered Mindy enough money to give up her own business and help Ryder run hers. Their partnership had proved to be an enormous success, and the horses kept coming in. They now had more offers than they could accept. There was no way they could get as many stalls at a single track as would be needed.

Ryder was sad to no longer ride Handsome Dancer professionally but took heart they would always have a special bond. Ryder would frequently take her most beloved horse out for long rides. They would go fast enough to give both of them a thrill. Reliving their tight bond and reliving their victories. Together. The wins were as much Handsome Dancer's as they were hers.

Handsome Dancer, although retired, showed no signs of slowing down. He had an even better life now than as an active racehorse, if possible, now that all he was doing was enjoying spa-like treatments and being bred. The mares that were lined up for him comprised a long list of equine beauties.

Ryder and Jake made sure to include in his list one of their own broodmares, Ice Palace. The bay mare was worthy of Handsome Dancer in every way, winning the majority of her races for five years straight. Ice Palace had already proven to be a great mom, too. Her first foal from a different stallion was only a few months old and obviously beloved by Mom.

Little Lenny loved Ice Palace's foal, too. Lenny would get up at the crack of dawn when he stayed by the stables to feed the ever-growing baby. In fact, Lenny had such a special bond with all the horses in their farm, Ryder knew he would one day grow up to be a horse whisperer. Like her. Jake teased their child's name should have been Lenny Phillip Doolittle instead of Lenny Phillip Carter.

Little Lenny had already picked out the name of the yet-to-be-conceived foal of Ice Palace and Handsome Dancer—Ice Dancer. He also anticipated, with much excitement, that one day he would be a jockey.

Her son grabbed her leg and gave her a squeeze. "Momma, I'm going to have lots of trophies, just like you."

Ryder and Lenny were interrupted when Jake walked into the library. He gave Ryder a quick kiss on her lips and held his hands out to the son who jumped into his arms.

"Wow. For a little guy," Jake marveled, "you're pretty heavy." He smiled over his shoulder at Ryder. "Looks like you've got competition," he said to her dryly. "Which one of you is going to win more racing trophies during their career?"

"I hope Lenny does," Ryder answered, giving both of them a kiss.

"I love you," Jake said, reaching his free hand out to take hers. "You've given me the loving family I never had but always wanted." He gave her the warmest smile, the heat reaching all the way to his eyes. "I must be a jockey too. I've been racing toward you all my life. I just didn't know it."

Ryder's heart melted. "I love you, too, Jake. You are the best prize of all."

Also by **Stacy Hoff** and **Soul Mate Publishing**:

DESIRE IN THE EVERGLADES

Stephanie Lang's successful career as a television producer can't give her everything she wants out of life. Her personal goals of writing a romance novel and finding true love languish. Emotionally scarred by her fiancé's affair with her cousin, she doesn't have the confidence to go after either goal again. At least she has professional confidence to fall back on; she is ready to produce the company's next hit show.

But when her boss reveals what the show is about, a survival documentary starring a sexy hunk, Stephanie's life is turned upside down.

Colin Brandt, billed as "The Evergladiator," will tackle Florida's Everglades with nothing more than his bare hands and a knife. Stephanie, instantly attracted to handsome, rugged, enigmatic Colin, worries he will not survive his twelve-day odyssey. If he does, he'll win a million dollars. If he fails, his beloved family's farm will go into foreclosure. Can Colin conquer the Everglades? And can he conquer her heart?

Available on Amazon: http://tinyurl.com/j33cxo8

LAWFULLY YOURS

The prestigious Connecticut law firm of Grovas & Cleval has always been rife with office drama and crazy clients. But an office affair between a young associate and a powerful partner—her boss—might be the biggest scandal of all.

Quirky, quiet Sue Linkovitch is Jordan Grant's newest hire. Barely out of law school and hired on a fluke, she has no idea what she's gotten herself into. Unfortunately, Jordan isn't sympathetic to her professional "growing pains." In fact, he's downright frosty. The only time he thaws is when he's around his five-year-old daughter. So why is she so attracted to him?

Jordan Grant sees Sue as bright, bookish, and a terrible temptation. Yet he knows not to get involved with a woman again-he learned this from his divorce. And if that hard-knock lesson wasn't enough, he's been falsely accused of sexual harassment in the past. If a colleague even thinks he's interested, it will be the death of his career—and hers.

Available on Amazon: http://tinyurl.com/gmerptw

DESIRE IN THE ARCTIC

Television producer Ana Davis's newest show is one she's forced to star in herself. Despite being a city slicker with no wilderness experience, she'll have to survive in the Arctic Circle for twelve days. The stakes are high. She could lose her very life. Good thing she's been paired with expert survivalist William "Redd" Redding, a mysterious, solitary, and very sexy man. Worse than snowstorms, predators, and a scarcity of food is an even greater danger—fighting off their attraction to each other.

Available on Amazon: http://tinyurl.com/gvphend

CPSIA information can be obtained
at www.ICGtesting.com
Printed in the USA
FSOW02n0156160117
29580FS